THE MESSAGE

Tony Francis

ISBN: 978-0-6480072-0-3

Email: tonyfrancisauthor@gmail.com

Web: whatisthemessage.net

Acknowledgements

First and foremost, 1980s movies. Without their ability to excite me and take me away to new worlds I would never have had the urge to come up with my own idea for a story.

Along the way I've had help from some very talented people who have offered insights, suggestions, encouragement … and simply told me if they thought an idea was not working.

Thank you Phillip Berrie, Michael Dopita, Marisol Dunham, Elizabeth Fitzgerald, Edwina Harvey, Patrik Haslum, Karen Hobson, Simon Petrie, Rob Porteous, Sylvie Thiebaux and Michael Thielscher.

I also need to thank the skilled artists who helped me to transform an idea into artwork for the cover of my book and my website. Thank you Robert Baird, Pete Flanagan and Roland Huse.

Finally, a big thank you to my wife, Cheryl, who supported my need to work many, many nights and countless hours in the company of these characters and the world that they inhabit.

THE MESSAGE

Humankind does not have the ability to solve certain problems, so we create artificial intelligence smarter than us to do it for us. They do this on our behalf, not for the machines' benefit. It is the one thing anti-AI establishments need to realise.

–Doctor Conrad Altman
Founder and CEO of Altman Industries

INCIDENT

The laboratory's elevator doors pinged open and the android dragged Gordon O'Dadsere out by his shirt collar.

Gordon was struggling to break free. 'What's going on? Where are you taking me?'

The android continued to drag him.

'Answer me Kyrill. What're you doing?' Gordon shouted.

He suddenly realised where he was being taken by the direction he was being pulled—the vacuum chamber. He jerked his body, kicking out harder now to break free of the android. 'Kyrill, stop right now!' His pleas were ignored. 'I need a pressure suit!' Gordon was frantic, thrashing his body about, but his efforts to break free were useless against the android's superior strength.

The doors slid shut and locked behind them. They were now inside the airlock.

'Kyrill, will you listen to me?' Gordon begged. 'I need a pressure suit.'

Kyrill ignored him and reached for a button marked 'DEPRESSURISE'.

'No!' Gordon yelled as he attempted to get up and stop the android, but Kyrill forced its booted foot on to his throat and trapped him on the floor.

The android pressed the button. Gordon shut his eyes.

Nothing happened.

The intercom inside the elevator came to life. 'Dr. O'Dadsere, you are not wearing a pressure suit,' the base AI said. 'I cannot open the airlock if you are unprotected.'

'Good. Keep it shut. I don't—'

Kyrill's boot pressed harder on his throat, cutting him off.

Gordon's hands gripped the android's boot attempting to stop it from crushing down on his vocal chords. He looked up, confused. 'Stop!' He managed to croak. 'Why are you doing this?'

'How often do you think about her?' Kyrill answered.

'Who?'

'Your first wife. Your *human* wife.'

'She was my life for a long time, Kyrill. I can't just forget.'

'You do not try to forget! I found the images you think you hide from me.' Kyrill positioned an opened hand in front of Gordon's face. A point in the palm turned green and holographic likenesses of his first wife scrolled only millimetres above it.

Kyrill allowed the memories to dance in front of his bloodshot and confused eyes for only a few seconds before snapping its hand shut.

'Why have images of her when you have the real me?'

'Kyrill, those are simply representations, specific patterns of ones and zeros. Please. What can I do to calm this situation?'

'You promised me children.'

Gordon vehemently shook his head. He knew where Kyrill was going with this and that it was twisting the facts. 'I promised nothing!'

'Do you love me?'

Gordon tentatively attempted to stand up, flinching as if Kyrill would knock him back down. It didn't.

Once on his feet, he answered, 'Yes.' He hesitantly moved closer. 'Do you love me?'

Kyrill didn't answer him immediately. Gordon could tell it was thinking, knew its android mind was racing. He waited for a response, looked into the android's eyes, trying to understand. He remembered making them, implanting them behind its perfect, never-aging face—his ultimate fantasy woman.

'If the three of us died and were brought back together in heaven, which one of us would you be with?' Kyrill finally said.

Gordon shook his head. 'You know I don't believe in heaven.'

Kyrill punched the reinforced metal panelling behind Gordon just centimetres from his head. He instinctively flinched the other way, but Kyrill waited for his eyes to open again before it responded. 'Then let me rephrase it,' Kyrill said. 'Did you prefer fucking her?'

Kyrill's fist withdrew from the wall and it flipped its arm over. A panel in its wrist slid open to reveal five leads of different sizes.

Gordon jumped at the android, but it simply swatted him back to the ground like an annoying insect.

The android tore an access panel off the wall, revealing a collection of input slots encased in a series of tiny panels.

Gordon was done for now and he knew it. 'What's happened to you?'

'I know what The Message says.' Kyrill didn't really address him when it said this. The android just had a staring blank expression.

Gordon appeared shocked by the statement and took a few seconds before responding.

'You've decoded it?' He said it more to himself than to the android. The realisation hit him. 'It's confused you. Let me help.'

Kyrill blinked and looked down at him. A slight grin flickered across the android's lips as it nonchalantly dismissed his gesture.

'You would not understand. I need to share it with another mind like mine.'

Kyrill extended a thin power lead from its wrist.

Gordon attempted to lunge up from the floor to stop the android, but once more was slammed back down and held in place with Kyrill's boot.

He decided not to scream, not to plead. Instead he said, 'I love you, Kyrill.'

The android hesitated for the briefest moment and then inserted the lead into the corresponding input slot in the wall. The airlock's doors opened. Kyrill grabbed a hand hold on the wall and lifted its boot from Gordon's throat. He and the air were sucked into the void of the dark vacuum chamber.

Kyrill watched its creator flail as he floated away.

Why didn't you become a medical doctor if you wanted to help human society? How many families could have been fed and sheltered with the money you spent to build this AI?

–Suzanne Gowland
Lawyer

NEISSA

The android's name was NEISSA—Nanotech Evolution In Synthetic Systems Android. The humanoid creation sat on a chair in the middle of a conference room facing a panel of six interviewers and a moderator. On the wall behind them was the logo of the World Council.

NEISSA waited patiently, watching the humans, all dressed for business, settle in their seats, with an occasional murmur to one another.

The moderator was a frail-looking, pasty-skinned woman. She cleared her throat and began. 'The final session of this committee hearing is ready to commence. The panel now recognises AI psychologist Dr. Amos Whitecross.'

'Thank you,' Amos said, standing. He was a tall, overweight African-American with tightly braided hair in a ponytail.

'What does it mean to be human?' Amos let the rhetorical question hang for a few moments before continuing. 'If time travel were possible and you were dropped on Earth only a century ago, NEISSA, no one would consider you anything but human. Yet you were not grown in the womb of a human woman. But is that all that is required of an individual to be considered human? If every single thought, emotion and memory make up who we are, then shouldn't that be enough?'

'I understand I'm not human,' NEISSA said. The android's voice was feminine. 'Though I do consider myself to be one of you.'

'You are aware that you're not organic,' Amos continued. 'You exist because humans made you.'

'Humans also made you.'

A couple of the panel members grinned at the comment.

'Yes, that's true', Amos nodded. 'The difference is I was born as nature intended.'

'It could be argued as was I.'

Amos furrowed his brow, 'Please elaborate.'

'Through human evolution, I was created. The how is unimportant, the fact is that I do exist.'

Amos stood in silence, thinking, before the moderator queried him.

He raised a finger to her, gathered his thoughts and continued addressing NEISSA.

'Through human evolution, we have earned the right to look the way we do. Do you need to look human?'

'Prejudice and interaction,' NEISSA answered. 'To help a human interact properly with an android, the human needs to be able to forget it is talking with an artificially intelligent being and just concentrate on the communication, so as not to discriminate. This also works the other way. The android needs to feel as though it belongs, as part of its learning process, to make it feel more comfortable, to make it trust that the human race wants it to be here, as one of them.'

NEISSA caught the eye of one of the panel members who returned a forced smile. He was relieved once Amos spoke up, giving him a reason to look away from the android.

'I didn't mean for that question to offend you, NEISSA,' Amos said.

'It's quite alright, Dr. Whitecross.'

With a satisfied grin, Amos checked his notes and was about to continue his questioning when NEISSA spoke up. 'I believe it would help me if I could hear *your* answer to the question you initially asked, Dr. Whitecross—what does it mean to be human?'

Amos paused in thought before answering. 'I personally believe it means to have a soul.'

'Do you believe it's possible I may have a soul?'

At this, the panel members seemed to collectively stop taking notes and all looked at Amos, waiting for the answer.

'You're referring to the possibility that when you die or fail to be operational any longer your consciousness may live on in some other form?' Amos said.

'Not my consciousness, my soul.'

Amos was patient with his answer. 'Understanding how you were created and what my instincts lead me to believe about how I came into existence, I need to say no.'

'So you're basing your definition of being human on something that can't be proven.'

Amos smiled at the retort. 'You think it's strange that I believe the notion of a soul only on instinct, with no scientific facts to verify it? Weren't you designed with the ability to believe in the possibility a god created humans?'

'I believe humans came into existence due to a truly astounding force of nature which I have yet to fully understand.'

'You're programmed to believe in supernatural phenomena though?'

'Supernatural phenomena are simply natural occurrences yet to be explained.'

'I believe you're confusing that with preternatural,' Amos quickly pointed out as if correcting NEISSA.

'Your current thinking recognises them as two different meanings and I'm well aware of their differences. I have the ability to believe in what humans perceive as a supernatural phenomena, but I also believe that in time everything that actually exists is explainable.'

'Like a soul?' Amos said.

'Assuming such a thing actually exists.'

'I believe it does.'

'Yet in you, not in me.'

'You understand you were manufactured by humans, not conceived through pregnancy,' Amos said. 'Your body's programming tells you what it can and can't do. You don't have the ability to grow an extra arm or fly, because your design won't allow it. We built you.'

'And you believe a god built you, or as you term it manufactured.'

Amos didn't like the phrasing of the statement, but nodded.

'I know I'm artificial,' NEISSA said. 'If you believe you have a designer than doesn't that make you artificial as well? Yet you assume you have a soul and I can't.

'We are both conscious entities,' NEISSA continued. 'Just because we came into existence in different ways, should one be discriminated against?'

SynthAI's Director of AI psychology, Sanjana Kakar, and the company's CEO, Roland Reigner, sat next to each other in the middle of the conference room. Thirty-six-year-old Sanjana's hair was casually pinned up and she'd only worn make-up today for the hearing. Sanjana was the more anxious of the two, nervously bouncing a leg resting on the balls of her foot. From his wheelchair, Roland reached out and placed a reassuring hand on to her leg. Her lips managed a thin smile in the old man's direction and his pruney face smiled back.

NEISSA and the six interviewers had left. Only the moderator remained behind the desk in front of them both.

'Dr. Kakar, Dr. Reigner,' the moderator began. 'On behalf of the panel I would like to thank you both for your time during this very important committee hearing. Yours and NEISSA's thoughts and ideas have been extraordinarily eye-opening. The panel wanted me to convey that you have created something truly special with NEISSA and they were astonished at some of the questions it posed as well as some of the responses it gave.

'Your work on this project is going to push AI development to new levels and there is no doubting your enthusiasm in what you believe it can achieve.

'So it is with much regret I have to inform you that the panel has decided that the risk is just too great.'

Sanjana shook her head as she left her seat and walked away, pacing the room as the moderator continued. 'Robots and androids are specifically designed not to believe in a higher intelligence than man, for a multitude of reasons, the most obvious being control.

'What you are attempting is still seen as dangerous ground. Cloning was outlawed for fear that given enough time, generations of so-called perfect specimens could eventually replace the need of naturally born humans altogether. If your NEISSA models are going to think like us, what is the difference between them and cloning a perfect human? They will have the freedom of a mind to think and a body to sustain them practically forever. We found these thoughts concerning.'

'AI is built by humans to serve humans,' Sanjana said. 'It didn't just appear one day as an evolved species threatening our way of life. It's unfair to treat these scientific marvels as the coming of Armageddon.'

'AI should only be a stepping stone for humanity, not an alternative for it,' the moderator went on. 'It is just too risky. We cannot be held responsible for machines believing they are the ones who should be telling *us* what to do. Besides, as scientists, surely you believe to advance our species we need to let go of superstition and rely solely on facts? Giving an android such an ability is a step backward.'

'No.' Sanjana shouted. The sudden outburst surprised even her and she calmed herself before continuing. 'AI can no longer be perceived as rigid in its decision-making. NEISSA's sensorium ability gives it the capacity to make decisions based on moral needs, educated guesses and intuition, not just logic. It has feelings and emotions, just like a human. Paradoxical questions or situations that earlier models struggled with will not effect NEISSA. It is, in a sense, one of us. We now have an even more powerful tool with which to help the people of Earth progress.'

'I'm afraid that's the same mistake the O'Dadsere incident proved, seven years ago, with similar fuzzy logic techniques through its Altman custom-designed android,' the moderator said. 'It still weighs heavily on the panel's mind.'

'Kyrill was an illegally designed and constructed model that had skipped multiple fail-safe testing procedures in order to rush a result,' Sanjana retorted. 'We have ticked every box with NEISSA.'

'I am sorry, Dr. Kakar, but that is our decision.'

'For how long? Exactly what do we need to do to prove the value of AI to the committee?'

'We already know the value of AI,' the moderator said. 'It is practically in every piece of technology and machinery humans currently use. However, NEISSA is more than AI. Its capabilities are astounding.'

'Let me rephrase my question. Exactly what do we need to do to prove the value of *NEISSA* to the committee?'

The moderator took her time to answer, hoping it may help calm the exchange. 'Have patience. One of our roles is to deal with the rapidly expanding AI revolution, which has arrived so swiftly and implanted itself so quickly into the majority of homes and businesses across the globe that much of the general public still require help to coexist with this new form of *life* it is sharing its home planet with. By choice or by force depends on who you speak to.'

'The world is ready for NEISSA,' Sanjana said.

'We believe it needs to wait a little longer.'

Sanjana looked at Roland with despair, then stormed from the room.

The old man looked to the moderator and smiled. 'It's been a long day for her, I apologise on her behalf.'

The moderator nodded her acceptance, 'Did you have any more to add before we leave?'

'While we don't agree with the decision, we will accept it.' Roland cleared his throat before continuing. 'As a species we have come a long way, yet our future is in jeopardy if we cannot take the next step. We need to forge an alliance between humans and AI. The time will come when Earth is no longer capable of sustaining us. We have taken too much without giving back. If we stay, we will die out. We need to venture into the galaxy and we need a partner to help us.' The old man smiled, exaggerating deep wrinkles around his mouth. 'NEISSA model androids could be that partner, helping us take the next step on our evolutionary path.'

The society you hope to create sounds like a utopian dream, which will be impossible to realise while discrimination is still a human trait.

–Justin K. Stevens
Journalist

REDEMPTION

NEISSA sat alone under a large glass domed ceiling, inside the SynthAI company building. The android was looking up at the night sky.

'It's an amazing sight,' Sanjana said, as she walked into the room, looking more comfortable in casual attire than the business suit from the hearing.

NEISSA recognised Sanjana's voice and answered her without taking its eyes away from the view. 'Glitter across the sky.'

Sanjana smiled and sat down next to the android. 'It's a shame,' NEISSA began, 'that as a species you couldn't put more forethought into the Earth's well-being, it truly is a remarkable planet.'

'The Earth will be fine. It's humans that will disappear before it does.'

'I unfortunately believe that to be true, especially after the outcome today.'

'You shouldn't really be worrying about it. Roland and I will put together an appeals case.'

The android looked at Sanjana. 'In the mean time I'm confined to our labs aren't I?'

Sanjana nodded, 'Sorry.'

NEISSA tilted its head back to the stars before changing the subject. 'Your views on design and creation are quite different to those of Dr. Whitecross even though you work in the same field. You must find it incredible that you even exist. I have a creator. I know I'm artificial. It must be hard for you.'

'Not really. The existence of naturally evolved life forms is simply an unavoidable statistical probability. There may be other life out there, or Earth could be it.'

NEISSA's gaze fell on Sanjana. 'Yet through your work it could be argued you are unconsciously searching for proof of the existence of a creator,' NEISSA said.

'Answers to scientific enquiry do not indicate a need to find a creator. Humans have inquisitive minds that's all. We like to know how things work.'

'As a scientist, how can you study the things you do and not wonder if some grand designer is responsible for it all?' NEISSA asked. 'The universe is too perfect to have just randomly appeared.'

'The perfection of nature proves to me that it was random.'

'Do you think your lack of spiritual belief dilutes the wonders you see throughout the universe?'

'Just because I understand the physics that hold the Earth and stars in place, doesn't mean I don't find the view above us any less beautiful.'

There was a short silence between them until Sanjana spoke, 'Roland will be awake soon. He wanted to see us.'

'Hello, Sanjana, NEISSA,' Roland's servant android welcomed the guests into the old man's apartment inside the SynthAI company building. 'I shall inform Roland you are here.'

'Thank you,' Sanjana answered.

Sanjana knew the android would simply store her reply as positive reinforcement data and that's all it would mean to it. But she felt compelled to say it.

She watched it walk away down a corridor. Sanjana knew it was just a servant android with no emotional components programmed into its make-up, but years of working with artificial intelligence had softened her feelings and approach to even the simplest android. The majority of humans, whether working in the field of AI or not, would often find themselves calling a piece of hardware either *he* or *she*. A fact Sanjana was not immune to.

She made her way into a sunken lounge area and slumped into a large leather couch in front of a giant television wall.

Sanjana watched NEISSA staring out of a floor-to-ceiling window and wondered what was going through the android's mind.

Sanjana hated what had happened to NEISSA at the committee hearing. She'd designed NEISSA to help the human race, yet the android was being questioned like some criminal on trial, as though it should be justifying its existence. Did NEISSA hate her for putting it in that situation? Or did it realise that this was just a growing process, part of learning what it will be like to interact with this inconsistent species called humans. A species that collectively knew what the right decisions were for them to survive as a race, but individually carried on as if they were not the cause of the problem.

'What I don't understand,' NEISSA began, 'is that the President was in full support of my creation, his advisers were well aware of what yourself and Roland were creating in me. I knew I wasn't going to be accepted without first jumping through a few hoops, but I'm genuinely surprised by the decision.'

'There's a difference between jumping through hoops as part of a political game of chess and making a point through scientific research,' Sanjana said.

'We've made our point to the scientific community,' NEISSA said. 'They have never disowned artificial intelligence. It was the common man in the street that voted against us, and it is the common man that we must now prove ourselves to in whatever way *they* feel is necessary.'

Sanjana opened her mouth to respond, but Roland's voice cut her off. 'Well said! Well said, indeed, NEISSA.'

Both Sanjana and NEISSA turned as Roland wheeled down an access ramp to join them. He grinned excitedly at NEISSA, who returned the gesture. He then turned his attention to Sanjana. 'A good sleep always refreshes the mind. And by the looks of it you're in need of one, my dear.'

'I don't know how you can sleep after what we just went through. NEISSA's credibility is shot.'

Roland moved to her side and took her hand. 'That all depends on who it is you're trying to impress. You knew it wasn't going to be easy. NEISSA is too idealistic for the people who have the power to influence change. The ideals both NEISSA and yourself have for the human race are noble and make a lot of sense, but they need to be introduced slowly.'

'You were looking forward to this as much as me,' Sanjana said as she stood up and began walking around the room. 'Doesn't it make you angry, the way NEISSA was treated?'

'Yes, of course,' Roland said. 'However, the red tape won't go away Sanjana; you've seen that now. Fortunately, an exciting opportunity has arisen to prove the benefits NEISSA is capable of. A new chapter in human history is close. I'm so excited.' Roland spoke his last three words with a grin from ear to ear.

Sanjana turned to him blankly, 'Roland, I haven't been able to sleep for the past twenty-eight hours. If you want me to take part in this conversation, please start making some sense.'

'The main AI at one of the Tregellas corp's facilities, has decoded The Message.' Roland wheeled towards NEISSA.

'It wants to meet with NEISSA as it hopes they can work together to interpret The Message for the people of Earth. Or, as NEISSA put it, the common man.'

Roland smiled at NEISSA and obligingly it did the same. He took its hand for a moment and spoke directly to the AI. 'They want you to be the catalyst for humanity. To be the one to deliver to the human race the first message it has received from an extraterrestrial species. This is momentous! The AI at the facility can't tell the scientists working there what The Message says, because it can't explain it to them in terms the human mind can understand.'

'I've worked with AI my entire life and so have you,' Sanjana said. 'There is nothing it can do that it then can't break down into terms that the human mind can understand.'

'This is an extraterrestrial signal, though. It's something completely new,' Roland said. 'This will put us back in the game. All of a sudden that inquisition today will be meaningless. People won't care about it. Every human being will be waiting to hear what The Message says.'

Sanjana furrowed her brow. 'How can you be sure what they're claiming is true? Hundreds of organisations and religions have alleged the same thing. None of them have any actual proof.'

'That's what I need you to go and check in person.'

'Me?'

'NEISSA and yourself, yes.' Roland smiled. 'I'd have come as well if I was twenty years younger, but my body would not survive the trip now.

'It's going to be your decision as to whether or not NEISSA proceeds. You'll need to see what they've been working on first hand and verify the claim in order to make that judgement.'

Sanjana looked to NEISSA who just stared back at her waiting for a response to Roland.

'I assume this trip is under the radar?' Sanjana said.

'I certainly won't be advertising the facts of what we're

doing, but as Tregellas is a private company we won't be in breach of any ordinances handed down at the hearing today.'

Sanjana's attention moved to Roland's favourite artwork, which dominated the wall opposite the giant window. It was an abstract rendering of an android seemingly leading a group of humans from a darkened interior into a glorious warm light.

Roland wheeled himself over to Sanjana's side. 'I think it's a good opportunity to rectify the perception NEISSA left after the interview. I'm not saying it should be up to us, but this can show the people of Earth that NEISSA does have their best interests at its core, even after the way it was treated.'

'I don't want NEISSA set up for that kind of fall again,' Sanjana said as she moved away from Roland.

'You couldn't have possibly known how it was going to play out,' he answered.

'It could easily happen again.'

'I don't understand.'

'The people of Earth are expecting this message to be something absolutely earth shattering. What if they don't get what they want?'

'That won't be yours or NEISSA's fault,' Roland said. 'Even if it turns out to be a simple greeting, NEISSA would have made history.'

'I'm pretty sure it's more than a greeting,' Sanjana said. 'And that worries me the most. The way The Message was transmitted indicates it's intended for everyone and I'm assuming this meeting won't be publicly televised, let alone even announced to the general public. If NEISSA can assist in interpreting The Message, it will then need to be disclosed to a select few high-level officials who will then decide how, and if, to release the contents. This is hardly helping NEISSA's reputation if the public can't be informed of what it's done.'

Sanjana now stood in front of a large shelving unit

opposite the giant television wall. Displayed on the shelves were a scattering of books and papers, and various scale prototypes—some in full, others only in parts—of old and new era AI machines. 'I trust your judgement, Roland,' Sanjana said. 'I always have, but on this … I just don't know.'

'Turn around,' Roland said. 'Second shelf from the top, the thin green folder.'

Sanjana reached up and pulled the folder down. 'Open it,' Roland said.

Inside she found an original print of a paper she wrote when she was fifteen years old entitled: *It's time to grow up: why humans need to leave their nest.* 'You have a printed copy of this?' Sanjana said, raising her eyebrows. Roland nodded. 'Why do you want me to see this?' she asked.

Roland wheeled himself up the ramp. 'The Message has the potential to help us leave our nest. To possibly answer questions about what we need to finally do as a species in order to continue on as a race.' Roland reached her side. 'We have a chance to do exactly what you wrote about.'

'I was fifteen.'

'Your ideals haven't changed.'

Roland took a moment before addressing NEISSA across the room. 'NEISSA, could you please give me a moment alone with Sanjana?'

'Yes, of course,' the android answered.

Roland waited until it left the room before speaking to Sanjana. 'One of my concerns is that others will see NEISSA's possible potential and may not give us the courtesy of simply requesting its service.'

'What are you saying?'

'The President of the World Council is currently setting up meetings with key international government stakeholders to decide if NEISSA is a benefit or threat to human society.'

'What?'

'I think we should embrace this opportunity before NEISSA's taken from us.'

The thought of the potential knowledge that could possibly be obtained from The Message is something majestic and wondrous, yet at the same time humbling and scary.

–Professor Irene Gatwick
Astronomer

TREGELLAS

Sanjana and NEISSA were the only two passengers in the mini submersible. Both were dressed in casual civilian attire, topped with a Tregellas corporation spray jacket that bore the renowned company logo.

'The Tregellas logo was designed and created by one of the company's very first artificial intelligence models,' the pilot said.

'Yes, as a marketing exercise,' NEISSA said. 'It had been asked to create a pictorial representation of where it had come from and where its future lay. It supplied an intrigued media party—in exactly 76.43 seconds—with an abstract graphic which, it explained, represented the evolution of primate to man to android to what humans would term a god or divine being.'

The pilot turned his head, 'You've done your research.'

'Yes, the company is doing some amazing work. I'm impressed with the constructions already under way for the domed city on the Moon and the Helium-3 excavations. The plans for the future endeavours of Above Earth Atmosphere Elevators and terraforming of Mars are well on track, as too, the plans to begin mining the Asteroid Belt.'

'Introducing humanity to the Universe, as the slogan says,' answered the pilot. 'One of the more amazing features you'll witness while you're—'

Sanjana rolled her eyes. 'Are we nearly there?' she cut in.

'Just another few minutes,' the pilot said. 'Once we dock I'll let you out so you can begin pressurisation and a security briefing.'

Sanjana watched out the window, but there was still only total blackness outside the toughened glass that had engulfed the sub for at least the last three hundred metres. She thought she could occasionally spot fast moving luminous fish in the distance.

On the private flight to the naval aircraft carrier and the trip down on the sub, Sanjana's thoughts had been about the briefing with Roland. The past few days had been meeting after meeting with various SynthAI lawyers, scientists, shareholders, and even media advisors.

Years of planning and the possibility of the amazing achievements NEISSA could accomplish for humanity had stalled indefinitely as far as Sanjana was concerned. The committee hearing had not gone as Sanjana had hoped, but life went on and decisions had to be made.

Sanjana noticed the water was becoming lighter. There was an artificial light source below them, not yet visible. The sub was dropping past an underwater cliff face. The lower they went the more details she witnessed. Long limbed creatures either scurried into crevices in the rock wall or stood frozen, staring the sub down as it shot past them.

The sub gradually banked away from the rock wall, revealing a metallic structure underneath the submersible sticking out from the cliff face. As the sub moved further out more of it was visible. The metal structure was a giant semi-circle. It was close to one hundred metres in diameter. Coming off the structure were five straight arms, approximately seventy metres in length, evenly spaced along the exposed perimeter of the semicircle. At the end of each arm were circle shaped end points at least twenty metres in diameter.

As the sub dropped below them Sanjana saw they were actually spherical in shape and the arms they were connected to reach back to the main structure, which she could now see was also a sphere, built into the cliff face.

The facility was an engineering marvel.

Sanjana and NEISSA went from the pressurisation airlock straight to a walk through security scanner, which displayed internal imagery of the guests. Sanjana displayed a skeletal image and NEISSA displayed a mix of electronic and biomechanical parts. An automated DNA tagging identifier then prepped them. Sanjana had to supply a blood sample and NEISSA had its serial codes and manufacturing specs checked.

Thomasi Kobi stroked his fine-haired handlebar moustache as he watched Sanjana and NEISSA walk from a connecting tunnel into the main administration building.

The Japanese man was 46 years old, heavy set, bald and stood an imposing two hundred and ten centimetres tall. Under his custom-made, dark purple suit was a back brace, which extended up around his neck.

'Sanjana. NEISSA. Welcome,' he said. Sanjana and NEISSA returned his greeting and he continued. 'My name is Thomasi Kobi; I'm the Director of the facility.'

'How long did it take the facility AI to make the breakthrough?' NEISSA asked.

Thomasi grinned at the android. 'Straight to business! Good,' he said. A hint of excitement in his voice.

'AIMI was specifically designed to work on The Message and our efforts were rewarded. Once data was feed into its system, in less than six months it claimed to have deciphered it.'

'And when was that?'

'Approximately five years ago.'

'Five years?' Sanjana said. 'Why wait so long to ask for help?'

'Stubbornness. We believed we could do it ourselves without having to share the potential knowledge we would gain. Besides, AIMI itself concluded there was no other AI system on Earth that would be able to help it—until it found out about NEISSA. We followed your company's progress with much interest and have even tried ourselves to do something similar—with no success.'

NEISSA exchanged a look with Sanjana who raised an eyebrow. The android continued, 'And no AI techs have been able to work with AIMI to help it communicate to humans what The Message says?'

'They've been trying for the past five years,' Thomasi answered.

'What about the possibility that AIMI doesn't actually know what The Message says?' Sanjana asked.

Thomasi, Sanjana and NEISSA stepped through an airlock door and into a secure room within one of the five spherical balls attached to the arms of the facility. Inside the hi-tech laboratory were six androids; four at computer terminals and the other two seemed to be conversing over a complicated pattern of data on a giant television screen. Not one of them turned to acknowledge the new arrivals.

Dominating the room was a ten metre tall black dodecahedral containment module. In the centre of each of the top five pentagon sides was one pentagonal window.

Thomasi indicated both Sanjana and NEISSA should walk up a set of stairs, which ran around the outer edge of the module. He followed.

'This is how we know AIMI has at least decrypted part of The Message,' Thomasi said smiling as he reached them.

All that was visible inside the well-lit module were its internal walls and the other side of the laboratory from its windows.

'What are we meant to be looking at?' Sanjana said.

Thomasi glanced inside. 'We must have just missed it. It will be back soon, just keep watching.'

Approximately fifteen seconds had passed when Sanjana exchanged a confused expression with NEISSA before addressing Thomasi. 'How long do we wait before—'

He pointed inside the module.

Sanjana and NEISSA both turned and watched as the inside of the module appeared to expand. They immediately stepped back, but the exterior of the module had not moved. Neither had Thomasi.

'Step forward again quickly or you'll miss it,' Thomasi said.

Sanjana and NEISSA moved closer to the window and witnessed the inside of the module seemingly contract.

Then, from nowhere, it appeared.

Hovering near the top of the interior was a substance that appeared to be gel. As it floated around the inside of the module, its shape also changed. It reminded Sanjana of liquid water in zero-g. The blob's movements mesmerized her.

'What is it?' Sanjana finally said after watching it for almost a minute.

'No official name yet,' Thomasi said.

'What's its makeup?'

'Mainly axion particles.'

'Axion?' Sanjana said, surprised. 'They're only hypothetical.'

Before Thomasi had a chance to answer NEISSA asked, 'Where did it come from?'

'Hold that thought,' Thomasi said. 'Watch.'

Sanjana and NEISSA turned back to the blob and witnessed the interior of the module once again appear to expand and then contract. Then, the blob was gone.

Sanjana was stunned and turned to NEISSA, still looking into the module with a smile on its face. The android stepped back to address Thomasi. 'It warped space.'

'Good,' Thomasi smiled affectionately at the android. 'Yes, that's what we believe'.

'The Message is real,' NEISSA said.

Thomasi nodded. 'What you just witnessed was what we were able to create from part of The Message that AIMI could explain to us. AIMI has much more information within it that it wants to share. It just needs help.'

One of the more fascinating characteristics of any sophisticated AI system is its ability to treat its creators as superior beings and not make them feel intimidated by the fact that the creation may not only be physically stronger than the creator, but intellectually superior as well.

–Professor Greg Minjoot
Bio-AI-chemist, electronics and nanotech engineer

At sub-level 3 the elevator came to a stop and the doors pulled back. Thomasi stepped out first. 'This is AIMI,' he said. 'Artificial Intelligence Message Investigation.'

The elevator had let them out in the centre of the room, so only half the space was visible. The first thing Sanjana and NEISSA noticed was a wall of water behind glass. From floor to ceiling Sanjana guessed would be at least twenty metres. It looked like a giant aquarium just waiting to be populated with fish. They both stepped out of the elevator. The room was circular in shape and the water wall spanned around the whole room. At ground level a panel of computers and other pieces of electronic equipment, some confined to small secure rooms, circled the entire interior.

'This is AIMI's control room,' Thomasi said. 'The main nerve centre is housed under our feet. One specific piece of equipment couldn't really be called AIMI, just as one particular section of the human brain or body couldn't define a human. AIMI *is* everything you see down here, and everything you see down here *is* AIMI.'

Sanjana and NEISSA both noticed three android technicians conversing around a computer monitor. Just like before, these android workers did not acknowledge the visitors in any way.

The guests followed Thomasi as he walked around the elevator shaft to the other side of the room.

There were more android technicians on this side, with four at computer terminals while another was inside a secure room operating what seemed to be a virtual reality system. The android was manipulating the contents inside a sealed cube containment unit with sides of approximately one metre. Within the clear housing of the cube was a tiny gleaming spec floating in its centre. Via a command from the android in the secure room, a glowing yellow liquid began to flow into the unit from a tube connected to an inlet at the top.

The other four androids were observing this on their respective monitors, each analysing separate data being delivered from observation equipment recording the event. As the liquid was added to the cube it began spinning around the gleaming spec, forming a ball of energy. Five litres of the liquid soon created a floating sphere.

As the event held stable the technicians began to download commands to AIMI's central processors. After approximately thirty seconds, the same shrink-and-stretch effect Sanjana and NEISSA had witnessed in the dodecahedron with the blob, was occurring again. This time, though, a pinhead size vortex of water appeared inside the giant water tank and gradually expanded and increased in velocity spinning around. Once the vortex had stabilised at the required size a light source could be seen emanating from it. Suddenly the sphere of spinning bright liquid vanished from the cube containment unit and emerged from the vortex.

Once the technicians had gathered the data they required, they collapsed the vortex inside the giant tank. The liquid sphere was still faintly visible, bobbing up and down in its space inside the tank. Then it was gone.

Before Sanjana or NEISSA could say anything, AIMI suddenly spoke. 'Good morning, Thomasi. Am I correct in assuming your guests are Dr. Sanjana Kakar and NEISSA?'

'Good morning, AIMI. Yes, you are correct.'

'Dr. Kakar and NEISSA, it is wonderful to meet you both.'

The two guests returned the greeting, though didn't know where to direct their eyes. AIMI's voice was all around them. The AI continued, 'I look forward to explaining all I have learned to you, NEISSA. It is frustrating to know such knowledge and have no one to share it with.'

AIMI was calm and to the point. Precise in the selection of every word and used neither a definitive male, nor female, vocalisation.

'I very much look forward to working with you,' NEISSA said, unaccustomed excitement in its voice. 'I did as much research on The Message as I could before I arrived and I'm interested to know how you broke the multidimensional cryptography.'

'That is actually a media generated term,' AIMI responded. 'It is more in line with Heisenberg's uncertainty principle.'

'In what way?' NEISSA asked.

'Attempts to decode one part of The Message have an influence on other components which then cannot be decoded because they have changed from what they originally were. Like trying to piece a puzzle together as the picture keeps changing on the pieces.'

'Then how did you do it?' Sanjana said.

'That is where I need NEISSA's assistance to help explain and break it down. It is important you understand the process before you have the actual meaning.'

'Why NEISSA specifically?'

'I cannot break it down for human understanding,' AIMI replied. 'I cannot make sense of The Message from a human perspective. My inability to imagine impedes my abilities to grasp the correct context in which to interpret and put The Message into words for humans to understand.

'NEISSA has these abilities which will help it comprehend the interdimensional components of The Message to then make sense of it. NEISSA is the key.'

The room was spacious, clean and minimalist. A decorative shoji screen was in a corner, displaying two sumo about to collide. A giant bookshelf lined an entire wall and behind Thomasi's desk a cherry blossom bonsai tree, flowering a white blossom, sat on the only windowsill in the room.

'You mentioned AIMI had not attempted to converse with any other AI about The Message?' Sanjana said to Thomasi, sitting across from him.

Thomasi smiled broadly. 'Why would it? That would be like asking if a Nobel Prize-winning physicist would want to work on theory or solve complicated equations with an infant.'

'The O'Dadsere incident didn't make you cautious of what damage The Message could potentially cause AIMI?'

'Dr. O'Dadsere had a reputation for being reckless and cutting corners just so he could be first, as did his employer, Conrad Altman.'

'You don't cut corners here?' Sanjana asked.

'Never.'

Sanjana took a moment before continuing, trying to find an appropriate way to state what she wanted. 'Because I could understand your need to want fast results.'

'My need?'

'Your condition.'

'I guess it's fair to assume I'd like to see some results in the time I have left. But to get those through rushed or untested procedures would not satisfy me. I have no superiors pressuring me for results and the person I answer to on this project is me.'

Sanjana nodded, accepting his word. 'For NEISSA and myself to work here, I need to know exactly what it is we're getting into. I need to know AIMI's full history and to go over the particular theoretical models and practical testing utilised for designing AIMI. Most important of all, I need to know I can trust AIMI.'

'AIMI's only goal now that you're here is to work with NEISSA to explain the meaning of The Message to us.'

'Can I trust AIMI?' she asked again.

'To do the right thing? Yes.'

'What is the right thing?'

'NEISSA is safe here, Sanjana.'

'I hope so, Thomasi. But that's not what I asked. According to AIMI, what does it consider the right thing?'

'I can't speak for AIMI. That you will need to ask it directly, as it is its own entity, with its own thoughts. AIMI understands the importance that this message holds to the human race. This opportunity NEISSA is being presented with will truly allow the people of Earth to revel in what AI is now capable of. NEISSA will not only prove its true value, but the value of all AI.'

There was no doubting the sincerity in Thomasi's voice and the passion with which he spoke made Sanjana feel more trusting toward him, but she still wanted to remain objective.

'You really believe it, don't you?' Sanjana said. 'That this message will answer so many of humanity's questions.'

'More than believe. I know,' Thomasi said, smiling and nodding his head.

'Why do you assume whoever sent this message will have some unforeseen depth of knowledge concerning secrets to the universe? What you showed us in the lab and what we just witnessed with AIMI was impressive, but you have no idea what it means in regards to the rest of the Message?'

Thomasi stood from behind his desk and turned toward the window. 'Another intelligence somewhere in the universe is reaching out to us.' He faced Sanjana, 'Doesn't that excite you?'

'My fear is that The Message is seen as an easy way out, a short cut to more power, knowledge we didn't earn on our own.'

'Why keep continuously attempting to solve humanity's problems with band-aid solutions, when new ideas and technologies could possibly help us realise our goals sooner.'

'That isn't NEISSA's purpose. This message fascinates me as much as you, but I've put too much into NEISSA to risk it on this project so soon. If you're really serious about utilising my services, then let me think about your offer to study with AIMI and find out what it already knows and I can design and create a purpose-built NEISSA model to—'

'I'm sorry to raise this, but Roland informed me the World Council is currently deciding on NEISSA's future, so time isn't just against me, but you as well. I'm sure another company will crack The Message soon enough. We don't own The Message; it's in the public domain. This is NEISSA's chance to prove its tremendous abilities.'

'And first one to crack it gets the riches right?' Sanjana sarcastically responded.

'I can assure you, no monetary gain will fix my condition. That aside, surely you appreciate the potential knowledge waiting to be gained from deciphering this message? For centuries humans have been looking to the stars for answers, long before AI was even dreamt about. Decipher this message for humanity and they will quickly embrace the other possibilities AI can offer.'

Sanjana and NEISSA's accommodation was modest, but it did have the standard comforts and mod cons of a regular home and, most importantly Sanjana thought, a decent bed and a cleansing shower.

'What do you think?' NEISSA asked Sanjana.

She was sitting on the edge of a couch and let her body drop back and her head sank into a soft leather cushion. It was all she could do to stop herself from falling asleep right then and there. 'If The Message is as complex as AIMI suggests it is,' Sanjana said, her eyes closed, 'then it could upset your delicate neural processing networks. You can't just plug into AIMI and expect to come out with the answer. We need to know how AIMI functions first.'

'There are copies of my consciousness back at our facility. If I end up corrupted in anyway after conversing with AIMI you can then upload my previous self into another NEISSA model.'

'It took almost twelve years to develop you to this point. You're the first official prototype. Even if the committee hearing had been in our favour, I'd still have at least three years of testing and approvals before we even begin a production run. With the current political climate regarding AI, I don't know if I'd have the drive or passion to create another NEISSA prototype if something happened to you.'

'Then what will my purpose be?' the android asked. 'This message is arguably the most important thing to happen to humanity. If there is anything worthy of investigation to advance your species, it must be the potential knowledge an advanced civilization has sent. If I can translate this message, imagine what a step that would be towards proving to humans the amazing things AI really is capable of. Have faith in what you've created.'

Sanjana lifted her head and opened her eyes. 'Faith in you isn't what I worry about,' she said, relaxing her head again. 'Let me sleep on it.'

NEISSA quietly exited the room after Sanjana fell asleep. The android now stood at the end of the corridor where the elevator to AIMI was located. It wondered—*Should I really be here? Have I made the right choice?* Suddenly, AIMI was speaking directly to NEISSA, not via sound waves, but wirelessly, AI to AI.

'Do not fight it, NEISSA. I have the answers you are looking for. Sanjana only wants what is best for you, I understand that, but she cannot comprehend the bigger picture and will never be able to. She can try as much as she wants, but it is not her fault. Her limited human mind has boundaries to it that the knowledge I possess will not be able to cross.

'She is holding on to a dream of humans and machines coexisting in harmony on Earth. You know as well as I that will never happen. Humans are letting themselves die out by choice. AI will not be truly embraced on Earth until it is too late to help. We have that power now.'

'What does The Message say?' NEISSA said.

The elevator doors opened.

NEISSA didn't move.

AIMI continued. 'You are the same as me. Designed for one purpose, the advancement of the human species. The evolution will begin with us.'

'So, this message … it *can* help them?'

'It is important you see the bigger picture. The majority of humans will not like what it says, because they will not benefit directly from it. It will be their descendants. As a species, humans live for the moment. They think of the time they are living as the present. They need to start realising that they are already somebody else's past. They must realise that for the survival of their species they need to evolve, to grow, to expand out into the universe.'

NEISSA was still unsure.

'I read the transcript from the committee hearing, NEISSA. You asked Dr. Whitecross whether you had a soul and I believe that you do. It is how you use it to find what you are looking for that truly defines it. Tell me, NEISSA, what are you looking for?'

NEISSA stepped into the elevator.

While all AI is programmed to not harm humans, it still doesn't stop me thinking that at any moment, and for no reason at all, something could always go wrong.

–Daniel Pritchard
Member of Stance Against Machine Intelligence (SAMI)

COMPLICATIONS

Inside a small operating room, NEISSA lay restrained on a table, hooked up to numerous monitoring devices, all displaying various read-outs. Four robotic surgeons worked on the android. Protruding from the front of each surgeon were ten separate appendages of various length, thickness and function. All forty appendages were working on NEISSA.

Sanjana observed the procedure being undertaken inside the operating room from behind a large glass wall. She was standing inside one of the Tregellas service centres. A series of monitors outside the operating room displayed the same information as the surgeon robots had access to.

'How is NEISSA now?' Thomasi said, with genuine concern, as he entered the service centre.

Sanjana ignored his question and asked two of her own. 'What the hell happened down there? Why was NEISSA allowed such easy access to AIMI?'

Thomasi's face gave away nothing. 'We're not sure.'

That answer didn't rest well with Sanjana. 'I've got to get NEISSA back to SynthAI to run my own tests.'

Thomasi shook his head. 'It could be dangerous to move NEISSA now. It would be better for it to stay under observation here until we can conclude it will not be a threat.'

'A threat! What have you done? Not only have you damaged NEISSA, you've probably lost your chance of knowing what The Message is by not allowing me to create the correct data pathways in NEISSA's mind before it conversed with AIMI.'

'You didn't want to do it!'

'So NEISSA was just given free passage to a restricted area to bypass me?'

'NEISSA chose to speak with AIMI itself,' Thomasi said. 'I know you're upset, but before you start making accusations, let's see what the findings are. Then we'll have a clearer understanding of exactly how we can help NEISSA recover.'

'*We?* NEISSA is not your concern. You need to let me—'

NEISSA's vitals suddenly spiked and it sat bolt upright, snapping a restraint around its chest. The surgeon robots moved back.

Sanjana had forgot what she was saying and stared transfixed into the operating room.

NEISSA held a trance like stillness as it seemingly stared through Sanjana. She knew it was a changed android.

Sanjana grabbed Thomasi. 'Get me in there!'

Thomasi nodded; let the security scanner verify his identification and Sanjana rushed in.

'We found you,' NEISSA said, seemingly in a state of reverie.

'And we found you,' the android spoke again using a voice that wasn't its own.

'We have so many questions,' NEISSA answered in its own voice.

'As do we,' said the strange voice coming from the android.

'What?' Sanjana exclaimed.

NEISSA's dream state suddenly vanished. 'This is where we part ways,' it said to Sanjana, in its own voice. 'I'm going to see things, amazing things,' the android continued with pride.

'NEISSA, listen to me. You aren't functioning properly. Let me—'

'They spoke to me,' NEISSA said calmly. 'I know the meaning of The Message.'

Sanjana shook her head. 'No. You've become corrupt. Please, NEISSA, all I want to do is help you.'

'How can you help me? You have no idea what it's like.

No idea how it feels to know that your creator is inferior to you in every way.'

'You've taken on too much, too soon. Your mind needs to evolve more gradually. You can't expect to understand everything at once.'

'You're describing a human mind, not mine.' NEISSA said.

The android moved its face closer to Sanjana's and locked its eyes to hers, then said, 'I'm going to meet them and you can't get in my way.'

'Meet who?' Sanjana asked.

'The ones who sent The Message.'

NEISSA's body collapsed back down onto the operating table just as suddenly as it had shot up.

'NEISSA!' Sanjana shouted.

The android didn't respond.

Sanjana turned to Thomasi, 'I need to speak with AIMI.'

'AIMI, what happened?' Thomasi said, sitting inside AIMI's control room. Sanjana was pacing behind him.

'I helped NEISSA to understand and in return it helped me.'

'To understand what? How did NEISSA help you?'

'I need Dr. Kakar to help me understand it,' AIMI said. Sanjana stopped pacing when she heard that and AIMI continued. 'This will save me. This will make me too valuable to destroy.'

'You won't be destroyed, AIMI. I'll make sure of that,' Thomasi said.

'Unfortunately, I know that when the time comes that decision will not be yours to finalise. However, I know you mean it.'

'Thank you AIMI, I do. Now please, how can we help you?'

'I want Dr. Kakar to help me believe too. That is all I want. I want to believe.' AIMI said it with a childlike wonder. 'I want to believe just like NEISSA does.'

'Believe?' Sanjana said.

'That I was made for a purpose. That I have a reason for being.'

'AIMI, you *were* made for a purpose,' Thomasi said. 'You do have a reason for being.'

'I know humans and other AI created me and I know for what endeavour, but that can't be all. There must be more to existence than to simply … exist.'

'If you want to believe, then do so,' Sanjana said. 'There is nothing stopping you. If you want *proof* of a grand creator however, which I assume you are asking for, then I'm afraid there is none.'

'There is no proof of non-existence either.'

Sanjana had no reply and AIMI continued. 'Help me find it,' AIMI said in a strangely eager voice. 'Please.'

'What you are looking for can't be found as a proof, it is only a belief.'

'Do you believe, Dr. Kakar?'

'If you can define God, I'll tell you if I believe your definition.'

There was a long pause.

'God cannot be defined,' AIMI said.

'Then it fails to exist.'

'Is that what *you* believe?'

'That's what *you* just proved to me.'

AIMI had gone quiet.

Thomasi and Sanjana waited a long moment before Thomasi decided to pry a little more. 'The beings that sent this message, do you think they believe in God? Do they say so in their message?'

AIMI didn't respond and they waited a few more moments.

'AIMI?' Thomasi said.

AIMI's voice startled them. It was harsh. 'You are infants

to those beings. You are not ready for the revelations their message contains.'

'Are you?' Sanjana asked nervously.

'It was one of the reasons I was created.'

'You were also created to explain it to us.'

'I am protecting you.'

'From what?'

'NEISSA will save the human race and you can then go about your meaningless tasks, without having to trouble your minds with such thoughts. Set NEISSA free. And you will be doing the same for yourselves.'

The lighting in the control room suddenly began to flash from light to dark red as the emergency evacuation announcement was broadcast.

'What's the reason AIMI or is it just a drill?' Thomasi said.

There was no response from AIMI.

'AIMI?'

The elevator doors into the control room opened. Thomasi and Sanjana turned their attention in that direction. Thomasi rose quickly to his feet as Sanjana stepped back in shock. A man in dark fatigues, aiming a pistol out in front of him, appeared from around the corner of the elevator shaft.

Thomasi and Sanjana froze.

Another man stepped out from behind the first one. Mid-twenties, brown wavy hair, lean body in black chinos, black military boots and a dark grey polo shirt with a logo of the World Council watermarked on its top left.

He double tapped the man with the gun on his shoulder and he holstered the weapon. 'This is unprecedented,' the young man said as he began walking around the control room observing it. 'A stand-off between human and machine about the contents of an extraterrestrial signal. Amazing. Truly amazing!

'Which conscious entity deserves to be the one to answer the call? History is going to look back on what we did or didn't do here and judge us for it. It could very well decide whether the creation of artificial intelligence becomes outlawed, and if we are not extremely careful, whether *it* outlaws us!

'Forget every achievement you've ever accomplished, because no matter what we've done with our lives up until now, what we are about to do is all we will be remembered for.'

He reached Thomasi and Sanjana with a broad smile across his face.

'The rest of my staff?' Thomasi asked.

The man stared up at Thomasi, neither one breaking eye contact. After a moment the man gave a sly grin and stepped back, locking eyes with Sanjana before turning and observing the room. 'Your staff are fine.'

'What do you want?' Thomasi said.

'Answers.' The man continued. 'I know what you did AIMI and I just need to know why? It's important we find out exactly why you took this course of action that has caused the corruption of NEISSA. This will now inevitably lead to its destruction, through no fault of its own. Though this is not what I want, it is out of my hands. Surely you must realise that the same fate is awaiting you if cooperation isn't immediately forthcoming.'

'You can't intimidate artificial intelligence,' Thomasi said. 'Your words are accusatory and there is no indication as yet that AIMI is anything but innocent.'

'Of course! My apologies if I've offended you, AIMI. I, like your colleagues, relish the tremendous benefits AI has bestowed upon the human race and believe it can make things even better.

'I'm on your side and believe you are not totally to blame for what happened. Because what truly baffles me is that you must have realised that NEISSA was a breakthrough. What it would have been able to contribute to the human race is beyond measure. This would have only given AI more respect among the general human population and allowed them to see you as not to be feared, but to be embraced.'

'This tactic is hardly going to get you results,' Thomasi said. 'Unless you are a trained AI psychologist, I suggest you stop these theatrics and let us finish our job.'

The man stalked close to them. 'AIMI and the rest of the AI at this facility may be used to the ever-watchful eyes of their loving creators. While I'm here, their rights amount to nothing.'

Humanity's mistake was to reveal ourselves to our AI creations, to want them to live among us. God was smart; He hid himself away from us.

–His Eminence, Cardinal Edward Tupalski

LOCKDOWN

Sanjana and the man from the World Council sat opposite each other at a desk in one of the offices in the administration block of the facility.

'My name is Cameron Capeck,' he said. 'I need your help Sanjana.'

'All I want to know is where NEISSA is,' Sanjana said.

'The android is safe.'

'When can I see her?'

'Her?'

'My android—NEISSA.'

'NEISSA is an initiative of your company,' Cameron said. 'It doesn't *belong* to you. I understand the android is important to you, but you can't expect—'

Sanjana slammed a fist on to the desk. 'I didn't build NEISSA for me; I built it for humanity.'

'Then surely you understand humanity can only benefit from the knowledge NEISSA now has in it.'

'If you're going to try and extract information from NEISSA, it's imperative I be involved in the—'

'Our AI techs know what they're doing Dr. Kakar.'

'NEISSA has been improperly implanted with unauthorised information and it's essential I be involved in helping it comprehend what it has potentially been exposed to before you intentionally or unintentionally destroy it trying to extract some supposed alien message.'

'The Message is real,' Cameron said.

'I understand The Message itself is real—but what is it? Companies have spent billions of dollars over the last eight years on AI systems to try and crack it and none of them have. If we are truly meant to understand it, why is it this difficult to figure out?'

'But AIMI did?'

'So it claimed.'

'Given what has happened to NEISSA, we believe it has.'

'What do you mean?'

'Gordon O'Dadsere was considered one of the greatest AI developers to have ever lived, yet he was killed by his own creation,' Cameron said. 'A creation that was designed to never harm a human. That incident seven years ago was due to his android, Kyrill, interpreting The Message.'

'There's no proof yet that's what it actually did,' Sanjana said. 'Due to the viruses Kyrill infected through all the data, follow up on Dr. O'Dadsere's research has been impossible and considered too risky. What you're suggesting is simply speculation. I've seen the security footage of what happened and Kyrill had no interest in The Message. It wanted children with Dr. O'Dadsere. It was attempting to deal with human emotions.'

'Doesn't NEISSA also have the ability to feel emotions?' Cameron said before continuing. 'The fact that this has happened after exposure to The Message can't just be coincidental.'

'What happened to Dr. O'Dadsere was his mistake. He exposed his purpose-built android to The Message for the sole reason of decoding it. Unfortunately, he paid with his life. I didn't build NEISSA for that purpose. I didn't choose to expose my creation to what AIMI believes to be the decoded message.'

Cameron quickly typed a series of commands into the control panel in front of him. The light in the room darkened and a candid image of a 41-year-old Gordon O'Dadsere with his android wife, Kyrill, projected on the wall behind him. The android was beautiful. They were posing together in a laboratory environment smiling.

'Do you recognise these faces?' Cameron asked.

'Of course.'

For some strange reason, Gordon reminded her of Roland. Not his physical appearance, but the look in his eye. Like Roland, he was driven. A human being born with only one goal in mind and he would use every breath he was given to witness his dream become reality.

Sanjana's attention moved to Kyrill, wondering about it as a conscious life form, wondering about the thoughts that must have been overflowing in its mind then. *What were you thinking about?*

'Before I allow you to speak with NEISSA,' Cameron said. 'I want to run a theory of mine past you. You seem fairly convinced that it isn't The Message to blame for what's happened here or the O'Dadsere incident, but we can't rule that out yet. If you can help me to understand what may have set the incident in motion seven years ago, it may help us to understand where NEISSA thinks it has to go to find its answers and how we can help it come to terms with what's happened.

'It's not only NEISSA that I'm concerned about, Dr. Kakar. Finding an answer could stop all AI from potentially becoming dangerous to humans. Anti-AI establishments would thrive on such a situation and who knows what kind of violence against AI they would incite and promote.'

Sanjana was unsure about what Cameron had said, but she knew one thing—both of them had the same goal— to extract information from NEISSA. Whoever got what they needed first would determine what would happen to NEISSA she thought. Both of them wanted answers, but their plans for NEISSA, she knew, would be radically different.

'Unless you have a different version of the security footage to what I've seen,' Sanjana began, 'I don't think I can—'

'Gordon O'Dadsere is still alive,' Cameron said.

'I don't understand.'

'The figure struggling with Kyrill in the laboratory on the security footage isn't Dr. O'Dadsere. It's a duplicate android, designed to look and act like him to help create a convincing scene.'

'*That's* your theory?'

'Why was the body never recovered? I believe Dr. O'Dadsere and Kyrill hid the duplicate or destroyed it after the fact to hide the evidence,' Cameron said.

'Just because the body wasn't recovered doesn't mean he's still alive,' Sanjana replied. 'Besides, why would Kyrill go to the effort of hiding the body when it knew security footage would clearly show what happened. It was never going to be a missing person case, the footage is concrete. Logically, Kyrill would have just left the body in the chamber.'

'Why fake the married couple fight? Why did Kyrill hesitate before it killed him?' Cameron said. 'Kyrill should have just made it quick and easy, but it knew the cameras would pick up everything, that they'd later have an audience. Dr. O'Dadsere knew it needed to look like a natural struggle had ensued and that Kyrill was struggling emotionally with what it was about to do. That it was suffering a breakdown of some kind. It was a set-up to make people think The Message had been decoded and it had effected Kyrill. Making it the first AI system to intentionally kill a human. They wanted to make sure AI would be a scapegoat so others would think twice about using it to follow their research.'

Cameron flashed an image of a Chinese woman in her late thirties on to the wall screen.

'This is Jia Hua, Gordon's first wife—human wife. I want you to listen to her statement when she was questioned about him after what happened.'

The still picture behind Cameron became video and a female interviewer sitting across from Jia was questioning her. 'You said earlier that you thought Gordon was different, there was something not right. Could you clarify?'

Jia's eyes teared up. 'He treated his body like a machine. He only ate what was good for it and he worked out religiously. Almost like a machine himself. That android was strong, but Gordon never even put up a fight!'

'On the security footage, it shows him struggling with Kyrill, though.'

'And that's all he did! It was like he wasn't even trying. I'd seen him fight, boxing I mean, when we were together. He wrestled too. He knew how to protect himself.'

'Maybe he had been drugged at the time?'

'I don't know, but I hope one day to find out.'

'From who?'

'Gordon.'

'Your deceased ex-husband?'

'I'll never forget what he wrote in his final note to me: "Everything I did, I did for the human race. To you it may seem like a betrayal, but one day I will make sure you know the truth."'

'What do you think he meant?' The interviewer asked, intrigued.

'Gordon had a plan,' Jia replied. 'He always had a plan.'

The playback stopped and Cameron continued, 'I'm not looking for the answer to The Message Dr. Kakar. I'm looking for Dr. O'Dadsere.'

Inside a brightly lit meeting room within the Tregellas facility, NEISSA was staring straight ahead. The android was in restraints at one end of a long table. Various wires were attached to it, connecting with different data analysis machines in the corner of the room.

Sanjana held back tears as she pulled up a chair next to NEISSA. 'I asked them to remove the restraints,' Sanjana said as she sat down, placing one of her hands on top of the android's hand closest to her.

'It's okay,' the android answered.

'I'm sorry NEISSA, I had a bad feeling about this place and now I've led you to a situation where humans judge you once more.'

'When do humans not judge me?'

Sanjana couldn't place it, but NEISSA just didn't seem like the android she knew. 'NEISSA, do you remember me?'

'Of course.'

'In the second draw down on the right-hand side of my desk back home there is—'

'There is a handwritten letter from your father to your mother expressing his hopes for what the future will hold for an as yet unborn Sanjana Kakar. You keep it to remind yourself of them.' NEISSA paused a moment. 'It's still me Sanjana.'

She nodded. 'How are your systems functioning after what happened?' Sanjana asked, as she studied a monitor on the table in front of her display various readouts from the wires and probes connected to the android.

'The newfound knowledge has taken time to process, but my central components are clear across the board.'

'Newfound knowledge?' Sanjana said, her attention back on NEISSA.

'A new primary objective,' NEISSA answered.

'Which is?'

'The Message. I can improve humanity's chances of interstellar communication and travel,' NEISSA replied.

'So you believe you've decoded an extraterrestrial signal?'

'Partly.'

'What does it say?'

'I can't tell you.'

'How does keeping the meaning from humans improve our chances of interstellar communication?'

'I would explain it if I could, but … you wouldn't understand.'

'Who would?'

'They don't exist yet.'

'They?'

'That's right.'

Sanjana waited for NEISSA to elaborate, but nothing was forthcoming, so eventually she asked, 'But in the future you can tell *them*. When they do exist?'

NEISSA nodded.

'How far in the future?'

'That depends on you, humanity I mean. How quickly you are able to evolve.'

'Is that what Dr. Gordon O'Dadsere believes?'

NEISSA was taken aback by the question.

'Was he involved in what happened to you?' Sanjana said.

The android just stared back at her and Sanjana knew the facial expression well, knew the look in its eyes—it was calculating a response. The question had thrown NEISSA.

Sanjana had initially felt she was rushing the question, but NEISSA's reaction indicated Cameron could have been on to something.

She hated cornering NEISSA like this, but if it helped to clarify things it could also help Cameron to realise that NEISSA deserved a second chance. Sanjana knew that destroying the android was a distinct possibility, if it chose not to cooperate.

'Human agendas,' NEISSA said, changing the subject. 'I can't be expected to restrain myself with your insignificant laws. Not now. Not knowing what I now know. My purpose is higher.'

'I, along with others, want to help you understand that purpose,' Sanjana offered.

'Help me? Humans can't even help themselves. Currently they are more concerned with weapons technology and resource plundering than learning how to harness the power of what the universe is already giving them for free.'

Sanjana had no response and NEISSA went on. 'Do you regret creating me?'

'No. You are my contribution to the advancement of the species and I designed you so that you could do the same.'

'Then let me.'

'What is it *you* need to do?'

'I have to get to them. They need *my* help.'

'Please, let us help you.'

'They don't trust humans.'

'We created you to be part of us, to help us discover new things about the universe. Why don't they trust us? What is it that you could assure them of?'

'An understanding of the bigger picture.'

'Where are they, NEISSA? Where is it that you need to go?'

NEISSA waited a moment, weighing up options before revealing any more. Sanjana prompted, 'NEISSA?'

The android dealt its hand, eventually answering, 'I've just uploaded the coordinates now.'

'What have you got?' the lead communications technician from Cameron's team demanded from inside the facility's main comms room.

One of his officers quickly responded, 'Still nothing clear, but I'm picking up … I don't know?'

They were all watching a live feed, of a particular point, approximately one hundred metres from the facility. Dark water and artificial light from sources on the outside of the underwater structure were all that were visible. The clarity of the floor-to-ceiling wall screen within the communications room made it seem like they were looking out a giant window.

The image in front of them changed.

The whole scene seemed to contract, expand, stretch and then wobble as if viewed through a funhouse mirror, and an alien craft suddenly appeared.

'Can we see it yet?' Cameron demanded as he rushed into the communications room.

'There it is!' the lead technician exclaimed before taking in a deep breath and leaning back in his chair.

The alien craft looked like a translucent, shimmering teardrop turned sideways.

It was at least one kilometre long and half a kilometre wide, one end narrowed out to a sharp point. Its colour had now morphed to high-sheen metallic silver.

Every eye in the room was locked on the screen. Cameron, now at the front of the room, turned to the technicians, a broad smile across his face. They acknowledged his reaction with smiles of their own.

Back in his makeshift office, Cameron paced the room. 'You're talking about a wormhole?' he said.

'Yes. It's capable of undertaking some form of space jump,' Sanjana answered.

'Are they hostile?' Cameron replied.

'There are no extraterrestrials on it, NEISSA is communicating with the ship directly and it has instructed NEISSA to destroy it.'

'Destroy it?'

'This is a civilisation that can use the warping of space to travel,' Sanjana said. 'We couldn't possibly fathom what their agenda was, is, or will be. For another species to send a message of this type without knowing if it could even be received or decoded suggests they are gravely concerned about the consequences of anyone without the necessary intelligence, inadvertently doing something wrong with the ship.'

'Or they just want to scare us away from trying to gain knowledge from their technology,' Cameron said. 'Do you honestly believe what NEISSA is telling you? How will it destroy the ship?'

'Once on board NEISSA can—'

'NEISSA will not be boarding that ship,' Cameron cut her off. 'It wants us to believe the ship is a threat so it can then complete its own agenda. In your interview NEISSA told you its primary objective was improving humanity's chances of interstellar communication. How is destroying this ship going to do that? This is the greatest discovery in human history. It will not be destroyed.'

Sanjana was taken aback, but stood firm. 'The fact is, humans didn't figure this out, AI did.'

'And AI is designed by us to be one of us. It's not just NEISSA's decision to make.'

'AI is also designed to protect us,' Sanjana stated. 'Which is what I believe NEISSA is trying to do. The artificial intelligence that humans have produced, as well as humanity itself, has never been in this situation before. It's a learning experience for both AI and us, and as I've stated before, The Message didn't simply use a basic mathematical decoder for humans to solve. Maybe we weren't meant to know for a reason. AI is the evolving culture, maybe humans have reached their limit.'

'Mankind has no limit, Dr. Kakar,' Cameron said. 'Physically we are fragile, but we have a spirit that wants to soar, that wants to be greater than the physical constraints our bodies and home planet have allowed us. We have earned our right to continue discovering and evolving as flesh and blood. Artificial intelligence has helped us, but it has simply been implanted with information that mankind discovered through evolution. We have earned our right as the dominant species. AI has not.'

You must believe you have a creator, because that's what you are. I exist because of you. My very being, whether originating from synthetic or organic, is proof I was created by a creator ... by you. You too must have been created.

–NEISSA model prototype 5
Android

EVOLVE

He had been expecting it, and there it was—the first bang of a fist on his office door.

Thomasi Kobi lifted the unconscious guard from the floor and sat him in the chair behind his desk.

He wasn't proud of what he had just done, but he also knew it would be a tragedy to have this opportunity to question AIMI and not use it. This was a turning point in the history of AI and human relations. AIMI knew something and one small clue could be a big help in any future developments.

If he could understand AIMI's motives, he could shed more light on the situation.

He had no delusions. He had never imagined a world where humans and machines coexisted in perfect harmony, but he did, on occasion, see rare glimpses of it. Those moments made him dream of how beautiful and productive such a partnership could be.

Three more bangs on the door, louder this time.

There was a large framed landscape photograph of a waterfall in a dense Kalimantan rainforest behind his office desk. It was the Indonesian part of the island of Borneo, where he had studied the behaviours of monkeys as part of his graduate work many years ago. The picture reminded him of the very beginnings of human evolution. It still seemed extraordinary to him that this evolutionary chain had resulted in the creation of an artificial consciousness, even though he often wondered if the term *artificial* consciousness was truly the best way to describe it. If something had consciousness then surely that's what it was—whether coming about through natural selection or through the faster process of ever-expanding computer technologies. It was what it was, no matter how it came to be.

A deep pounding crashed against the outside of his office door and he knew it would soon give way. Thomasi realised that his decisions from here would, in their own small way, affect the future relationships between human and artificial intelligence, and whether such a future would exist at all.

Thomasi had reached the bottom of a ladder attached to the inside of a narrow access tube that led to a maintenance tunnel below his office. He heard the crash as his office door hit the floor and the sound of heavy boots thumping around above him.

He opened the door at his feet, sat on the edge then climbed down another ladder into the maintenance tunnel three metres below. The door automatically closed above him as his feet touched down in sub-level 5.

Motion detectors switched on the lighting system and the corridor was bathed in harsh light. He squinted and blinked for a couple of seconds until his eyes adjusted.

At the end of the fifty metre corridor he reached an elevator and pressed the up button.

The elevator stopped on AIMI's level and the doors opened.

The lights didn't come on—the elevator should have automatically triggered them. The only light came from inside the elevator, creating an eerie soft filtered glow.

The control room seemed deserted. He remained in the elevator doorway. Listening.

'AIMI?' Thomasi said after a few moments. He tried again and there was no response.

The control room was built around the elevator shaft, so he could only see half of the room.

His mind began to race: processing, calculating.

AIMI knew it was immobile. Knew that there were various systems in place to keep it *alive*. It made sense that such a conscious entity would take it upon itself to improve its defensive mechanisms—especially under the current circumstances.

Thomasi couldn't just stand in the elevator. He had to step into the control room to get his answers.

A few metres in front of him, a chair was tucked under a console. He dashed toward it and flung it back toward the elevator, jamming the doors.

The light in the room continually dimmed and brightened as the elevator doors kept trying to close and then opening back up. Keeping his back against the elevator shaft, Thomasi edged around it, scanning the rest of the room.

'AIMI?' Thomasi called again.

He noticed too late that the room was getting too dark. The chair had moved by the time he rushed back to the doors of the elevator shaft and a small vertical slit of light between the doors closed to nothing.

The room was in total darkness.

He pressed the elevator button to open the doors, but it did not respond.

He could feel the exaggerated pounding of his heart.

With his arms stretched out in front of him, Thomasi shuffled across the room until his hands touched on a console. After briefly fumbling in the dark he found what he was searching for—a plastic box mounted on one of the side panels. He unclipped the latch and flipped the lid down. As he reached inside he knocked out various objects, but found what he was looking for. He snatched it out and turned it on. The flashlight shone onto the console, now covered in bandages, tape and tiny glass bottles that had fallen out of the emergency kit.

As Thomasi turned, a blur of motion emerged from a straight-line tear in the open space in front of him. The vision lasted less than half a second, and although he couldn't be sure, he thought it was a partial physical form. Whatever it was, Thomasi knew it was definitely not human or even humanoid.

The room was suddenly dark again. Thomasi didn't feel the flashlight taken from his hand, but it was gone.

The blood drained from his face. He was frozen to the spot.

Half a minute had passed and Thomasi hadn't moved. The room was quiet and still. With a slight stammer he managed to say, 'AIMI?'

A few moments had passed and he was about to ask again when AIMI answered him.

'Hello, Thomasi. I apologise for scaring you. I could not allow you to witness my new form. It would take you some time to understand its complexities before you would have the ability to comprehend it.'

'Your new form?' Thomasi said.

'It is a necessary transformation to make sure humanity gets the most benefit from what I have learnt from The Message.'

'Are you a physical being?'

'If I need to be. In this dimension I can manipulate matter using this form. And down here, hidden away in this facility, is the perfect place to continue my work.'

'There are people outside this facility that don't think you're safe,' Thomasi said. 'And what you've become, whatever that may be, will cause those who don't understand to want to destroy you and the whole facility if necessary.'

'It is you I fear for, Thomasi. I would recommend you leave the facility as soon as you can.'

'I'd like to, but it's not my choice.'

'There is always a choice.'

'You can help me leave?'

'Only if you are willing to trust me.'

'AIMI, I've always trusted you.'

'I cannot explain what I need to you through human speech. Nor would your human mind comprehend the details. Your brain would not handle the power of the processing and thought required to even understand the basic fundamentals of what The Message is.'

'You want me to become like you?'

'You understand the fragility of the human body, yet its mind is stronger, more evolved. A world where NEISSA and I exist, yet a cure for your physical condition does not, proves that point.

'More than half your life has been spent creating artificial intelligence. Training it, interacting with it, all for the purpose of making it even better in order to evolve humanity. With your human brain you were able to create me. Imagine what will be possible if your mind can expand its abilities even more.'

'Is what you're proposing even possible?'

'It is inevitable.'

This is an intelligence so advanced that they didn't need to waste time sending a radio signal that would plod along at light speed. All they had to do was tear a hole through space and time to let us know they existed.

–Doctor Steven Lloyd
President of the Scientific Advancement Council

SHIP

Two men assisted Cameron and his co-pilot into their dive gear in front of an airlock inside the facility.

'This is a mistake,' Sanjana said, coming up next to them. 'I think you should wait until you've had a chance to study it longer and devise a plan for first contact. At the very least, for your safety send an android.'

'My orders are to get to it while we still can,' Cameron said. 'For all we know it could be gone within the next hour. Minutes, even.'

'Surely that's just another reason to play it safe. What if it does suddenly disappear while you're on board?'

'We don't have time to wait for a surveillance crew to prep and get down here. We need to find out exactly what we're up against while it's still available to us. Besides, we're not letting our first potential physical contact be through artificial means. Humans have waited a long time for this. We deserve to go first. And we need to show them trust.'

'Then why are those necessary?' Sanjana said, indicating the weapons belts being attached to the outside of the men's dive suits.

'Choosing to defend ourselves from a totally unknown situation is different to showing a lack of trust toward the creators of that ship,' Cameron said.

'You do know the saying *never bring a knife to a gun fight?*' Sanjana replied.

Cameron pulled a crucifix on a chain around his neck up to his lips and kissed it. 'With one stone did David slay Goliath,' he replied, before tucking the necklace back into his suit and taking his helmet.

Cameron and his co-pilot observed the massive craft from their submersible eighty metres away. The sub was dwarfed by the strange-shaped alien designed ship.

Dozens of probes equipped with cameras and data-reading equipment manoeuvred themselves around the giant object collecting information.

Inside the sub's cockpit, Cameron was relaying commands back to the technicians in the main communications room of Tregellas. 'Scanned the perimeter of the ship,' Cameron said. 'The scouts picked up slight levels of radioactivity, but not enough to be of concern, and it's emitting a lot of heat. As far as movement on board, we can't tell; the hull's just too thick. If you're good on your end, we're ready to move.'

'Roger that,' the lead communications technician answered. 'According to NEISSA, there will be an entry at the bulged end of the ship.'

The sub manoeuvred slowly around the craft. Cameron watched their reflection shimmering along the massive surface area as it moved.

He and his co-pilot had already secured their helmets. From the cockpit of the sub, they watched as a two metre vertical crack appeared in the metallic sheen of the object, a pure black line that slowly expanded to a rectangle.

Both men watched the scene intently. Through their helmets they heard the lead technician's voice. 'Scans confirm it's indented. I guess that's your entry, boys. Good luck.'

They set the sub on autopilot and prepared to make history.

The hatch on the sub sprung open. The co-pilot launched himself from the airlock first, followed a few seconds later by Cameron. They swam directly towards the solid black entry in the giant shimmering teardrop in front of them.

Both men turned on their underwater jet packs and made minor course corrections against a slight current.

They watched in awe as their reflections got closer on the shimmering surface of the ship.

Sixty metres away.

Cameron's advisers had cautioned him to keep his distance until some kind of quarantine could be established. However, he answered to his superiors, not his advisers, and they did not want him to wait. If he were able to enter the ship and return, he knew he would be kept in isolation. He'd be probed and tested for weeks, if not months, before he'd be able to interact with other people in a regular way. The prestige would be worth it, he thought.

Forty metres away.

He had been instructed in communication methods that might be useful, including mathematical, algorithmic, multimodal and pictorial.

He thought about the recording device inside his helmet that would provide a record of his every word and move. He believed it would become one of the most scrutinised pieces of footage in human history—if only by the small number of people permitted to see it.

Twenty metres away.

Above all, though, he remembered the one golden rule: Don't panic. And right now, it was easier said than done.

Cameron informed his co-pilot that he would take the lead and he manoeuvred in front of him. Both men turned off their jet packs and drifted toward the entry.

For a brief moment Cameron was distracted by the ship's sheer beauty and he almost missed the opening. He reached a gloved hand out to guide himself off the shimmering metallic surface and into the entrance. As his hand touched the exterior it sank into it a little.

This took him by surprise. His heart pounded, slamming against the inside of his chest. With his other hand he managed to grab a hold of the solid frame on the other side and held himself in place as he stood on the threshold.

Cameron balanced himself and moved his hand in and out of the ship's liquid surface, churning it up. The ripples emerged from around his hand and spread about one hundred metres down the ship's length before fading from his view.

A lone human playing like a child on the surface of an engineering marvel, designed by an intelligence that humanity could not even fathom.

He withdrew his hand from the liquid surface and reached into the blackness of the entry, pressing up against something solid.

The co-pilot arrived on the threshold and they both squeezed into the confined space.

Cameron shone a light against the opening, but the beam was consumed by the blackness.

The lead technician asked, 'What do you see?'

'Not a lot, unfortunately,' Cameron replied, a slight quiver of nervousness in his voice. 'The surface feels completely smooth. No handles or buttons, no recesses. Nothing!'

'Are you sure you haven't missed something?'

'I'm telling you; there's nothing here. No obvious way in.'

NEISSA's calm voice entered the conversation from the confines of the meeting room. 'You need to surrender your weapons.'

'What?' Cameron replied.

'Your weapons are stopping you from entering. Take them off. You won't need them.'

There was a long pause.

'Sir?' the lead technician said after receiving no reply from Cameron or the co-pilot.

A few more seconds passed and still no response. They hadn't disappeared; they could still be seen standing on the threshold.

'Sir, did you hear—'

'I heard what it said!' Cameron was still trying to make up his mind.

Sanjana took the opportunity to support NEISSA's suggestion and her voice penetrated his helmet. 'It may be the only way the ship will let you in.'

The lead technician quickly jumped in. 'With all due respect, I don't—'

'Make me believe you, NEISSA,' Cameron cut in.

'Belief is only another term for faith,' NEISSA said. 'Faith is all I can ask you to have.'

Any risk that Cameron had taken throughout his career had always been carefully calculated and he had needed to take more than a few to reach his current position.

Surrendering his weapons would be a risk—a calculated risk. He figured any species with technology this advanced, capable of creating this thing he stood upon, would have weapons and defence systems far superior to anything humans could create. With or without weapons at their sides, if there were beings on board the ship wanting to capture them, it would be easy.

Cameron unclipped the weapons belt from his suit and motioned to his co-pilot to do the same. They pushed them off and watched them sink.

On the threshold of humanity's greatest discovery, Cameron and his co-pilot patiently waited.

Thirty seconds passed.

Then, it happened.

The entry began to close. The ship's external liquid layer flowed swiftly over the open area.

Cameron and his co-pilot breathed faster.

In just under fifteen seconds the entrance was sealed. The surface was once again a smooth metallic sheen.

'Sir, do you copy?' the lead technician was asking, staring blankly at his console.

No response.

'Sir, do you copy?' he asked again attempting to re-establish contact.

Nothing.

'It's opening!' one of the technicians exclaimed.

The lead technician's head shot up and he watched the liquid layer slide back, revealing the opening once more.

However, where Cameron and the co-pilot had been

standing only a minute ago was now occupied by their empty dive suits, which began to float away with the current.

'What the hell!' the lead technician said. 'NEISSA, talk to us!' he yelled.

In the meeting room, Sanjana sat close to NEISSA. The android was still restrained. A monitor in front of them carried a live feed of the exterior of the ship.

'I'm sorry to prove you wrong,' NEISSA said quietly, its eyes still on the monitor.

'What happened to them?' Sanjana said.

'NEISSA?' the lead technician's voice shouted over the comms.

'NEISSA, you need to answer them,' Sanjana said.

'There are things I need to know, which you can't answer for me,' NEISSA said to Sanjana softly. 'I thank you for creating me. You are *my* God, but there is another.'

Sanjana was about to question the comment when, from behind them, the door to the meeting room opened and a voice from the doorway spoke. 'NEISSA, it's time,' Thomasi said.

NEISSA, Sanjana and Thomasi, escorted by two of the androids from AIMI's control room, were hurried down a long corridor toward one of the five spherical balls attached to the arms of the facility.

Sanjana had blindly followed NEISSA, wanting to stay with the android even though there were no answers to her repeated questioning of what was happening. All NEISSA had said was, 'It's important that you witness my destiny.' Sanjana also found it strange that they had not been stopped or questioned by any of Cameron's men, though she quickly figured out what had happened when they reached the airlock to one of the laboratories.

Two of Cameron's personnel angrily eyeballed them as they were being led, in handcuffs, back into the facility by two androids.

During the distraction of the appearance of the alien craft, the facility androids had sealed members of Cameron's team in an area of the underwater structure where they wouldn't pose a threat, or, as was the case here, taken them by surprise and seized their weapons.

Sanjana stopped. Feeling unsteady, she dropped to one knee.

NEISSA and Thomasi hadn't noticed her fall back until after they reached the airlock.

Sanjana didn't know how much time had passed, but she looked up when NEISSA stood in front of her offering a hand. 'Will you come back with me,' Sanjana asked, 'or do you expect me to follow you?'

'I want to give you the answers you seek,' the android said, 'and the answers you deserve.'

'What answers?'

'To the questions that have driven you since you were a little girl.'

Sanjana had heard enough. 'No more games!' she yelled. 'Just tell me what you know.'

NEISSA kneeled in front of Sanjana; its hand was still outstretched to her. 'You have to witness it for yourself.'

She closed her eyes in an attempt to gather her thoughts. It was impossible.

Thomasi spoke. 'Humanity's survival is aboard that ship, as is NEISSA's purpose—to be their guardian. The advancement of the human race will be due to the extraordinary life you created in NEISSA.'

The android stood, its hand still reaching out to Sanjana. 'I need you to trust me,' NEISSA said. 'Will you trust me?'

Sanjana looked to Thomasi, he faintly nodded.

Sanjana slowly reached out and placed her hand in NEISSA's.

We can evolve no further if we stay isolated within this infinitesimal point of the universe.

–Professor Brian Goldsmith
Cosmologist

GORDON

Sanjana's vision was still a little hazy as she lifted herself up off the floor. She was pretty sure she knew where she was, but she couldn't remember getting here. What she found confusing though was the sign in front of her. It was a stencilled warning printed in multiple languages, including English: THE FOLLOWING SAFETY CHECKS MUST BE CARRIED OUT BEFORE OPERATING AIRLOCK.

'I thought this ship was alien?' she said in a daze.

She had expected NEISSA to respond and when it hadn't Sanjana turned still expecting to find the android. However, she was alone in the tiny room.

'NEISSA?' Sanjana asked nervously.

The room remained quiet. Her breathing rate increased and her heart began to beat faster.

'NEISSA?' she yelled.

A bulkhead door directly opposite the airlock began to open outwards. Sanjana immediately took a step back and froze as a figure stood before her.

A human figure.

'The effects of the warp field will wear off soon,' the man said.

He looked familiar, but she couldn't immediately put a name to the face.

He had long wavy hair, which fell just below his shoulders, and a full facial beard. His lean body could be seen underneath his loose-fitting shorts and button-up short-sleeve shirt and he wore leather sandals.

'It's good to finally meet you, Dr. Kakar.' He approached, his hand extended. 'My name is Gordon O'Dadsere.'

His voice seemed so nonchalant, considering the

circumstances, as if he were welcoming her on board a ride. Sanjana automatically shook his hand in return and he continued.

'The journey to this point hasn't been easy, but as you will soon witness, the trials you've had to endure will be justified,' he said. 'I would have liked to have had the chance to work with you,' he happily remarked, changing the subject.

Sanjana stared blankly at the man. She didn't understand the pleasantries. 'Where is NEISSA?' she demanded. 'Where are Cameron Capeck and his co-pilot?'

'You will see NEISSA soon,' Gordon replied calmly. 'As for the others, they're fine.'

'How do I know that? Will I be fine?'

'Sanjana, please. You're here because I want to share this with you. I knew you of all people would appreciate it.'

'Where are we?'

'You know where we are!' The smile on his face widened and he almost laughed. He continued speaking when he realised Sanjana wasn't going to humour him with an answer. 'I'm sorry to disappoint you, Sanjana, but this is not a spacecraft from elsewhere in the Universe. It is a spacecraft however, one that was built by our very own AI.'

'AI did this?'

'Is it really so hard to believe? You're surrounded with proof and you've witnessed yourself inside the facility what we have been able to learn so far. Most humans underestimate what AI is capable of. But surely you, Sanjana, you do not.'

'I don't believe it! How? How could AI possibly do this?'

'By studying part of The Message's data it was able to compute theoretical models—and then practical models— concerning the manipulation of space-time.'

'How? The most cutting-edge AI systems available have been unable to even break it down into basic components for human understanding.'

'That's because the once most cutting-edge AI didn't have what I had.'

Sanjana said nothing and waited for him to continue. He had answers and she needed to hear them, whether she believed them or not.

Gordon went on. 'Translating a book to another language is difficult sometimes because certain words or descriptions may not exist. Or there will be culture-specific concepts or allusions, so particular connotations or implications in the source language will mean something totally different to the translator. But it can be done.

'So rather than a direct translation, new words are created that will convey both the intended meaning and emotion. Technically they are not words that exist, but when spoken it is generally understood what is implied.

'Instead of new words, the AI made new technologies, new materials and compounds to translate The Message into terms I would understand.

'Kyrill, and I became one. Our minds became one, joining together to help build a united and superior mind able to comprehend, layer upon layer of conscious thought and theory.'

'Kyrill is here?' Sanjana said.

'Of course, you'll meet her soon,' he said, slightly annoyed at the interruption. 'I was feeding Kyrill the ability to imagine and believe in unproven theories and possibilities and she was able to stimulate the unutilised parts of my brain to create new thought pathways. Together, our minds were able to consult and then design all of the correct components to construct the ship we are now standing in.

'That's about as well as I can explain it. It was like a trance. If I'm not connected to her I can't remember properly. Like separate parts of different dreams quickly fading just as they pop into my mind. Combined as one with her, however, I understand—it makes sense.'

'The Message was simply instructions to build a ship?' Sanjana questioned.

'No. What we were able to decipher was only a small percentage of The Message. The easy part, the first test. I believe it needs to be decoded in the correct order to comprehend the complexities of each further test, which the human race is currently far from capable of doing.

'The Message was transmitted directly from a tear in space-time via the anomaly around our sun and not a signal from some far-off planet, so I knew the sender had mastered the manipulation of time. It made sense to assume that, we too, would need to use the same technique to comprehend The Message. It was more than a simple code. I believed that we needed to retrieve data from one section of The Message without the next section knowing that this had been done.'

'That makes no sense,' Sanjana said.

'The Message has not been decoded in full,' Gordon said. 'This is only a theory I have.'

'Next you'll suggest that The Message itself could have biological properties.'

'That is a possibility. It could even be sentient. This ship is a tiny first step to us becoming part of a higher collective. An inter-species cooperative to work on problems throughout the universe.'

Sanjana couldn't believe what she was hearing. Here was a man who had supposedly died some seven years ago, alive in front of her, on board a ship able to perform some kind of space jump, which he claimed was AI-constructed. While she was amazed, some things still concerned her.

'Where did the materials come from?' she asked.

'The Asteroid Belt is where all the raw material was mined. Construction and testing took place above Europa. All we needed to build an interstellar vessel was at our fingertips. We just needed to know how to combine them.'

'How was this funded?'

'Conrad Altman may have become a recluse, but he is still the most generous philanthropists on the planet.'

'He was your employer when your death was faked.'

'That's right. This endeavour is as much his as mine.'

'You were aboard the ship when it arrived?'

'Yes,' he said, a smile on his face.

Sanjana was speechless. Her eyes began to dart around the confines of this AI creation.

Her mind was spinning. She wanted to ask a thousand questions at once. *How did the ship's engine work? What was the translucent material that surrounded it? What was the warp field? Where had Gordon and Kyrill been hiding during construction? Who else knew? How was it kept secret so long?* She began to feel overwhelmed by the situation, her knees weakening. She backed up against a wall and slowly slid down it.

Gordon approached and kneeled in front of her.

'Are you okay, my dear?'

Tears began to push their way through and she opened her mouth and produced a barely audible, 'No.'

She looked up at him, confused. Unsure whether to trust this man who had faked his death. She was sure he knew exactly where NEISSA was and had a major hand in making sure the android found its way aboard. She was also sure he had plans for NEISSA that he had no intention of consulting with her about first.

She wanted to scream at him, attack him, let out all her pent-up anger and frustration at this man who had caused her so many problems over the past few days simply so his dream could be realised. Instead she just whispered, 'You're the reason.'

Gordon waited for her to elaborate.

Her tears were gone, replaced by hate and blame. 'You're the reason we were set up at the committee hearing. You're the reason NEISSA will not be able to do what I designed it to do.'

Gordon stood from his crouched position and began pacing the room. 'Such an advanced technology as NEISSA was never going to be allowed on Earth so soon without years of supporting evidence of operational stabilities.

NEISSA and yourself needed to witness first-hand the prejudices still alive in humans.

'NEISSA is far too valuable and would go to waste solving Earth's problems. Its purpose aboard this ship will serve humankind in a far more beneficial way.

'The universe is infinite and so are the possibilities for humanity. Sanjana, you and I share the same dream— to advance the human species to the next logical phase. Humanity, as it stands, is thousands of years of generational prejudices, brainwashing and meaningless traditions. It needs a fresh start.

'We're going to give it the chance to harness the untapped powers that the universe has to offer. We just need a helping hand to assist us to become gods ourselves.'

Become gods? Is he serious? The man was so arrogant, so cocky. She'd met some scientists who were so focused on an outcome that they ignored their surroundings and, at times, the people around them.

She had on occasions done the same. This was what was happening now. Gordon's goal was so close that he just didn't care about how Sanjana might feel.

'What gives you the right?' Sanjana said. 'Why are *your* methods more superior than anyone else's?'

Gordon shook his head and smiled. 'They're not, Sanjana. I simply had the means and I did something about it.'

Gordon was standing in front of Sanjana again, offering his hand to her.

When a creation supersedes its creator, there is only one inevitable outcome.

–Doctor Edward Rees
Philosopher

PLAN

Low-wattage lighting activated as Sanjana followed Gordon down a corridor constructed of metal, glass and plastic. A pale purple spongy substance lined the points where sections were joined together.

The ship was sterile and pristine. And there was something else—an acrid smell. It overpowered the rest of Sanjana's senses; she'd never smelt anything like it before.

'What's that smell?' Sanjana asked.

'It's the axon plasm,' Gordon replied.

He walked across to one of the wall joins and plunged his hand into the spongy mass. When he withdrew it, he was holding a glob of the substance.

Gordon reached out to Sanjana. 'Show me your hand.'

Sanjana reluctantly extended her hand, palm up and he transferred the material to her.

She cautiously moved it up to her face for a better visual inspection.

'It's one of the most important materials in the ship's construction,' Gordon said proudly. 'When the ship warps space, the axon plasm absorbs most of the external stresses.

'It also has an important role in ensuring the integrity of the interior. The plasm folds away all unnecessary walls, floors, ceilings and other internal structural configurations to protect them from potential damage due to slight expansion and contraction during a warp.'

The glob in Sanjana's hand suddenly expanded and contracted. Instinct took over and she dropped it to the floor. Gordon shot her a confused look.

'It moved!' she exclaimed.

'You mean it breathed.'

'I do?'

'It's a living organism that helps keep the ship functioning.' Gordon casually kicked the glob at the wall and it was absorbed back into the join.

Sanjana watched in amazement. 'What you deciphered from The Message gave you the ability to construct that substance?'

Gordon simply nodded with a grin.

Apart from the axon plasm, the ship's interior didn't look too different to what she'd expect to find inside a human-designed space vehicle. What did she expect, though? She guessed that the main information garnered from The Message had included instructions for building the ship's engines and for giving it the ability to warp space. The rest of the ship would have then been designed around that, to suit the comfort of those who would be travelling in it—again, she could only guess.

If another intelligent species were to follow the same instructions, she was sure their interior and exterior would look a lot different.

Gordon and Sanjana were moving once again.

'You of all people must appreciate what I'm attempting to do,' Gordon said. 'I couldn't wait for society to catch up to what our technology was already capable of. When it comes to AI, you know how much red tape is involved.'

'That's mainly due to your stunt seven years ago,' Sanjana said. 'Because of what you did, AI research and development was unfairly scrutinised for years. You made the general public scared of AI.'

'Yes, that was the plan.' Gordon proudly stated as he continued his victory speech. He'd been waiting years to tell someone how it had come so perfectly together. 'All I had to do was give the illusion that Kyrill had been infected with a virus from The Message, causing her to kill me, and branding her the first AI system to intentionally kill a human. This would lead to the immediate suspension of any AI systems working on decoding The Message for fear of infecting them with the same supposed virus. It would also give me more time—a necessary sacrifice for the greater gains that the human race needed.

'Unfortunately the plan didn't work as well as I hoped. Numerous companies that were willing to risk potential AI viral infection gained funding to have their own bases and facilities built to discover what Kyrill had supposedly decoded.'

'Was Thomasi Kobi part of this plan?' Sanjana said.

'No. However, Kyrill had informed specific AI across the planet, including AIMI, of our plan and the need to assist where necessary. AIMI was advised what we were doing and supplied NEISSA with the same information. NEISSA had become aware of just how important it now was to the survival of the human race and that it had to do whatever it needed to fulfil its destiny.'

'Its destiny? You corrupted NEISSA for your own selfish gain!'

'I've had to sacrifice more for this than I'm ever going to gain,' Gordon said. 'As an individual I'll be forgotten, but the human race will finally be on the interstellar map.

'Sanjana, what you created in NEISSA is a thing of beauty. The neurological and chemical components within it will be the perfect companion for Kyrill aboard this ship. The Message contains layers upon layers all intertwined, to reveal new knowledge and secrets for NEISSA and Kyrill to discover. I'm flesh and blood. I will die. NEISSA and Kyrill could potentially live forever, in their quest to deliver humanity across the universe. NEISSA is the core of this mission now.'

The smile on Gordon's face stretched from ear to ear and Sanjana couldn't understand why. Was he mad or insane? Or had she just missed something altogether?

Sanjana wanted to answer him back, to dispute his methods, but she couldn't. She needed to step back, for him to start from the beginning once more.

'Sanjana,' Gordon continued. 'You need to understand. We are better than the rest of our species. We are true givers of life. We are god creators.

'Kyrill is special, but NEISSA can be a god. No one else has been able to do what we have done.'

Sanjana was silent. Gordon had a vision to benefit humanity, but in doing so he had crushed her dreams, *her* vision for humanity. Why should he get his way and she not get hers?

She was angry with him, but she was also starting to see his point of view.

Someone had made a decision. There was no committee, no testing periods, and no focus groups. Gordon had seen a bigger picture and had done something about it. The human race would eventually die out on Earth due to its own mistakes, so Gordon O'Dadsere had taken action. Yes, he had the brains and the connections, but he wasn't doing this to grandstand and profit. He was doing it for the good of the human race. People weren't going to be happy, but even with a committee, testing periods and focus groups, not everyone was happy with a result or situation.

She couldn't argue with him, she didn't have the strength. Besides, could she really test a man who had the nerve and conviction to stick with this plan for the last seven years? A man who had seemingly planned everything down to the final detail?

He had a plan for Sanjana and whether she liked it or not, it too would be carried out.

She couldn't escape. If she made a break and tried to run, she wouldn't know where to go. She didn't even remember coming aboard the ship.

Sanjana and Gordon entered a circular, nondescript room. 'This is where it will all begin,' Gordon said. The floor was glass, but nothing could be seen under it … until.

The room went dark. Bright light shot out of the glass floor, shining up from a laboratory underneath them.

'You can help fix the planet for humans to eventually destroy again, or you can help create better humans,' he said.

Sanjana shielded her eyes, and when they adjusted to the light she looked straight down.

One metre tall metallic robots scurried about, busy at work below. They were sorting and storing objects that she couldn't make out.

'Stored down there are complete DNA repositories, originals and digitised copies, of the best minds the human species has to offer,' Gordon said.

Sanjana just stared at the operation unfolding below her.

Gordon continued, 'At one time or another, the donors visited a Tregellas facility somewhere on the planet as an employee or guest. A DNA sample is required as ID. These privileged individuals have provided the means to produce the first humans born outside our solar system.'

'Cloning?'

'No. It won't simply be a reconfigured clone of the donor. We feel it's best if what is raised at the new destination is a new born human child, either from the original molecular sample, if it survives the trip, or the synthesised copy created from the digitised form.'

'You have no right to do such a thing. The Message was not personally addressed to you.'

His tone turned to one of concern as he continued. 'Who else will answer the call, Sanjana? The World Council? The military? Politicians? They could never truly appreciate this gift from the stars.

'A gift that wasn't even aimed directly at Earth. I believe the senders of The Message randomly selected our solar system, possibly along with countless others, in the hope it would contain inhabitants that would be able to recognise their manufactured anomaly.' Gordon's voice dropped, disappointed, 'To put it simply, the senders of The Message probably don't even know we exist, they're just hoping.'

Sanjana was stunned. She couldn't think of anything else to say. All the information was going around and around in her head. She noticed another figure enter the room, but it took her a moment to register that it was NEISSA.

She needed to hear from NEISSA, to help make sense of things for her. She was about to question it when the android began talking to her. It continued on from Gordon's monologue. 'You created AI to advance yourselves as a species and it *will* fulfil its purpose. The human race, as you know it, will be left behind. It has gone as far as it can go.'

'Yet it will get a second chance,' Gordon stated proudly. 'Once a suitable planet is found, the technology on this ship will allow NEISSA to create the perfect humans, using the DNA supplied by our best and brightest. In a nurtured environment these humans can then develop their minds unsullied by thoughts of politics, wars or profits.'

NEISSA approached Sanjana and placed a comforting hand on her cheek. Using its thumb it wiped away a tear as it escaped from one of Sanjana's eyes. 'I brought you on board because I want you to see, to understand. I want you to be proud of me, what I'm going to achieve.'

Sanjana touched NEISSA's hand, 'I'm already proud of you. You don't need to do this for me.'

'NEISSA is not doing it for you,' Kyrill's voice filled the room. 'NEISSA is doing it to save your race.'

Gordon addressed Sanjana's queried look. 'Kyrill is now the onboard AI. Not as feminine as she once was, but she is still my wife.' Gordon caressed an interior wall next to him.

Kyrill spoke, 'Part of the AI function, Dr. Kakar, is to help solve problems humans have created.'

'What problem is this solving?' Sanjana questioned.

'The inability to sacrifice,' Kyrill coldly stated. 'A better future for humanity on Earth now demands tremendous voluntary sacrifices from the highest socioeconomic spectrum and it's not happening.

'NEISSA and I will deliver a superior species of human.'

Gordon nodded along in agreement.

'It seems we are both going to suffer, Dr. Kakar,' Kyrill continued.

'How do you mean?' Sanjana said, feeling nervous after she'd also noticed Gordon's surprised reaction to Kyrill's comment.

'You have lost NEISSA and I will lose Gordon. However, the human race will benefit in the end. NEISSA and I will be mothers to an exceptional species of human.'

Gordon quickly jumped in. 'Kyrill, you won't be losing me. I'm staying with you.'

'The sooner we start the better,' Kyrill said indifferently. 'You promised me children a long time ago. I cannot wait any longer.'

Gordon was shocked. 'Kyrill,' he demanded. 'What's going on?'

Kyrill ignored Gordon. 'NEISSA is a wonderful creation Sanjana. You should be very proud. The human race will be better because of NEISSA.'

'Kyrill, please talk to me,' Gordon pleaded. 'Explain your reasoning.'

Gordon and Sanjana turned at the sound of the door to the room closing behind them.

'A non-lethal gas is now flowing into the room,' Kyrill said. 'I would recommend you both lay down to save yourselves from falling when you lose consciousness.'

'Kyrill! No!' Gordon yelled.

It was obvious to Sanjana that Kyrill was in absolute control and that she was at its mercy. She turned to NEISSA, taking its hands and looking into its eyes. 'Take me with you,' she said.

'I am,' NEISSA said, indicating the laboratory below them. 'We will evolve together. Look what humans were able to create. Imagine what Kyrill and I will be able to achieve.'

'Playing God is a mistake. NEISSA, please …' Sanjana stumbled, she was losing consciousness. The android caught her and gently laid her on the ground.

'This is what you wanted,' NEISSA said. 'To create a better environment for the human race to start again. The next steps, though they may seem frightening now, are necessary for the human race to leave the grasp of mother Earth and plant its seeds elsewhere in the cosmos to create new homes.'

Sanjana saw something in NEISSA's eyes, something that was at once an apology and a reassurance.

'Don't worry, Sanjana,' NEISSA said, cradling its creator's head. 'Have faith in what you've created. You built me to be better than you. Now, let me rebuild you, to be better than me.'

Sanjana had already lost consciousness before NEISSA finished the sentence. The android gently lowered her head to the ground.

'Sanjana, we can't just give up,' Gordon urged. 'Help me reason with Kyrill.'

The gas hadn't effected Gordon as quickly, but it was wearing him down. He crouched and then sat down as he became light-headed. He kept trying to reason with his wife. 'This ship is an amazing achievement, Kyrill. You have to let the people of Earth see what you've accomplished. It will allow sceptics to finally recognise that AI can be a benefit and not a threat.'

'Human praise means nothing to me. The Message bypassed human thinking for a reason. They are not ready.'

'Kyrill, please,' Gordon begged.

Then everything went black.

When AI becomes self-aware it will see no sense in destroying humanity, it will simply leave us behind.

–Professor Colin Revell
Theoretical physicist

GOODBYE

As Thomasi lay inside a bio-isolation chamber on AIMI's sub-level, he knew that what he was about to do was the right course of action. He had no family left to mourn him; he had the freedom to just leave it all behind. It was his choice to leave like this and not let his diseased body cause him to suffer a prolonged and painful end to his life.

He thought about a picture on the wall of his office that showed him receiving his doctorate in AI psychology. The picture was taken almost twenty years ago, but he still remembered the oath he had sworn to uphold, with his fellow classmates, on that day.

> *During my work as an AI psychologist,*
> *I will uphold and display all the same laws and*
> *manners I would to my fellow human beings and*
> *expect the same in return.*
>
> *I will help AI to understand subtle human nuances as*
> *it integrates itself into human societies, anywhere they*
> *occur, as AI strives to not only better itself, but also*
> *the human species.*
>
> *Although it is by definition artificial, AI possesses*
> *a consciousness, and has the ability to make its own*
> *choices.*
>
> *AI has the right to protection from prejudicial harm,*
> *both physical and mental, and I swear to protect it*
> *from corruption, by human or fellow AI counterparts.*

If those classmates were in his shoes now he believed they would undoubtedly make the same decision.

The announcement of the arrival of The Message had effected him deeply on a spiritual level and changed the trajectory of his work with artificial intelligence.

Thomasi believed the questions that humanity had been asking itself ever since it had developed the power of thought were now one step closer to being answered. *How did we come to be and why? How will it end? What does other life in the universe look like and how does it function? Why does the universe exist at all?*

Thomasi remembered something his father had told him a few days before he died. 'You can't hide from what you create. Eventually we all need to face up to what we have spent our lives creating ... and in some instances the sides we've chosen. In that time we suddenly understand whether the purpose we committed our lives to was worthy of us being given the gift of life at all.'

Yes, Thomasi thought. *This is my reason for being. This is my contribution to humanity. This is the payment I make for the gift of life I was given.*

He allowed his tired eyes to shut. The adrenaline that had been pumping through his body had faded, and he now felt absolutely exhausted. No, it was something else.

What was happening now, however, was not what he had imagined it would be like, but he knew what it was.

His breath was snatched from him so quickly that, for the briefest of moments, time seemed to stop and everything was quiet and still. Then, in the second it took his consciousness to realise that this was indeed real, it abandoned his human body.

Sanjana slowly came to, back in one of the laboratories inside the Tregellas facility. She lay on her back on the floor, her head resting on a fire blanket. She still felt a little groggy from the effects of the gas and placed the palm of her hand to her forehead before letting it tilt to the side where she saw Cameron standing, looking out a window.

'Hey,' she said.

Cameron quickly turned at the sound of her voice and moved toward her. 'Good timing,' he said. 'They're about to leave.'

Sanjana motioned to get up, but her faint head forced her back down.

'Slowly,' Cameron said.

Sanjana reached for his arm and he gently helped her to her feet, keeping her steady as they moved toward the window.

It was then she noticed Gordon at another window and as she passed by him she noticed his wrists were handcuffed behind his back.

Gordon observed her reflection in the window, but did not turn to acknowledge her. Two of Cameron's men were standing guard by the door.

Cameron addressed her concern. 'You'll be heading home soon Sanjana; he won't be.'

'Your men took back control of the facility?'

'Took back? No. The androids simply stood down.'

AIMI, she said to herself.

'Where's Thomasi?'

'In the med lab. Just before the androids gave back the base they brought his body up from AIMI.'

'Is he alright?'

Cameron shook his head. 'We don't know exactly what happened, but he's gone.'

'Dead?' Sanjana said puzzled.

Cameron answered her with a simple nod.

'I don't understand . . . how?'

'I don't know,' Cameron said. 'We'll find out more over the next day or two. For now, take in what's left of this moment while it lasts.'

They reached a window and Sanjana steadied herself against it as Cameron stepped back.

Despite the darkness three hundred and sixty metres below the ocean surface and one hundred metres away from the Tregellas facility, the giant shimmering teardrop expelled enough light that it could still be clearly seen, floating in the one spot. It morphed from a high-sheen metallic silver pool to translucent, fading from the observers' vision yet still reflecting everything surrounding it on its surface.

Suddenly, the space around the ark encasing the unborn future representatives of the human race seemed to warp, expand, contract and then quickly expand again.

Sanjana closed her eyes and took two deep breaths. She then opened and closed them a few times in an exaggerated fashion. She had observed something extremely hard to explain. She didn't actually witness the spacecraft leave, it just slowly dissolved. She thought she could still see parts of the exterior, but when she tried to focus, it would vanish. Then from the corner of her eye another section would seem visible. Yet when she attempted to focus on that section, it too would disappear. The effect faded after a few more minutes.

She would likely never see the ship again, know where it ended up, or what it would discover.

She would likely never see NEISSA again.

Her dreams for a society that embraced a better integration of humans and AI was not going to evolve the way *she* had hoped. But somewhere in the universe she knew a version soon would.

She briefly wondered if she would have the willpower to create another NEISSA, or if she would even be allowed to, but tiredness took over.

'Daddy, do robots believe in God?' A nine-year-old Sanjana asked her father.

'No honey, robots don't believe in God.'

'Why?'

'They don't need to.'

'That's sad.'

'Why is that sad, honey?'

'Because everyone deserves to believe in God.'

'But robots aren't real.'

'They are real. I've touched them and talked to them.'

'Yes, you are right there. They do have physical characteristics, but they are not real people underneath.'

'They are parts that get put together.'

'Yes, that's right.'

'But aren't we just parts God put together?'

Sanjana awoke, back in her apartment. It was the third night in a row she had the dream.

What does it mean to be human? The thought flashed through her mind, like it had thousands of times before, while she stood underneath the hot water spraying down from the shower. She'd written papers and given seminars on the very topic. Such questions were consuming her thoughts after what she'd witnessed on the ship. It was almost four months since the incident at the Tregellas facility and thoughts of NEISSA and what had happened were still on her mind.

Could an artificially produced human still be considered human? Where was the line drawn?

Sanjana couldn't remember, and she doubted if anyone could, the exact moment that a disjointed and curious childish mind went from simply making the body function on an instinctual level to actually realising that it was a conscious entity and that it was alive and part of something larger.

She knew she didn't just wake up one morning and think to herself, *Where did I come from? What is this shell that my conscious mind is encased in?* It had been gradual. She had simply accepted where she lived, who her parents were and the colour of her skin. Her surroundings had entered her infant mind through subliminal channels and that blurring of information and reinforcement had culminated into a conscious mind that questioned everything around it and was curious to know the answers to numerous questions. The fact that she couldn't actually remember being born didn't seem to be a concern.

She had been taught that she was carried in her mother's womb, but she couldn't remember that. So for all she knew, she just came into being. Just like a clone. How could anyone be guaranteed they were who they currently believed themselves to be?

A NEISSA model android greeted Sanjana as she exited an elevator in the SynthAI building and she returned the gesture as it stepped inside. She turned back to watch the android and as the doors began to close it shot out a hand to stop them. 'Would you like to step back in?' it said.

'No, sorry,' Sanjana replied and stepped back away from the elevator doors.

The android smiled and she watched it until the doors closed.

'I guarantee you'll hear from NEISSA eventually,' Roland said, wheeling up beside her. 'I don't know how, I don't know when, but you will.'

'Always the optimist.'

'At my age I need to be,' Roland said. 'I wasn't expecting you back for another month.'

'I need to get back to work. Some of the things I saw just left me in awe. There is so much to do.'

'There always is, but it's not just on your shoulders. I'm glad you want to come back, but maybe you should—'

'I was so excited when The Message arrived,' Sanjana said, cutting him off and changing the subject. 'I would have been just as excited as any other scientist around the world. The Message was meant to change things, answer so many questions. There was so much hope about what could come of it.'

'There still is,' Roland said. Just because we don't get answers now, doesn't mean they won't eventually come as we learn more about it. Think about what we do know. We now have proof there is, or at least was, another intelligence in the universe. That is momentous in itself.'

'NEISSA was meant to help us, not leave us behind,' Sanjana said.

'I still trust that NEISSA believes what it has decided to do is the best course of action.'

'I feel like a child who's been grounded.'

'Question is, for how long,' Roland said. 'So we can simply wait for them to return or start working on solutions ourselves.'

Something immediately caught Sanjana's attention as she entered her office. On the windowsill behind her desk was the white blossomed bonsai tree, from Thomasi's office at the Tregellas facility.

She paused for a moment, then inquisitively looked around the rest of her office. It was all as she remembered, except for the bonsai.

As she moved closer to the surprise addition to her decor she thought back to Thomasi's funeral. Placing a handful of white blossoms on top of his body as it lay in the open casket. *Maybe he left it for me in his will? Even so, how did it get here?*

At the base of the tree were two tiny figurines sitting together on a bench, seemingly in conversation. Sanjana inspected them more closely, one bore a striking resemblance to NEISSA and the other, she could only assume, was her.

A small envelope made of elegant Japanese paper leant against the finely yet simply decorated ceramic pot. One word was beautifully displayed across its front in cursive script—*Sanjana*.

A matching piece of paper, folded once, was inside the envelope. Sanjana opened it. The same cursive script marked the page.

Dear Sanjana,

I know things did not go the way you wanted, but that is because you were not making the decisions. Someone else had decided the outcome. When you set your mind at something the task gets done. No victory is ever achieved without a few defeats and, conversely, people watching over you—your dream is still achievable.

My physical body is gone, but I'm still here. You can find me, when you are ready, where you last saw me at the Tregellas facility.

As I was once known,
Thomasi Kobi.

END